CW01501486

CHAPTER 1

"Why do you need to take another vacation?" her boss asked. "You just took one." He shook his head, looking irritated. "You know how anxious I get when you're not here."

More like, her stingy-ass boss didn't like having to pay a temp. Losing cash made him anxious. It had nothing to do with her not being there.

She pushed out a breath, trying not to look or sound upset, because she sure as hell *was* feeling a little upset. "I took two days a couple of weeks back." *Two measly days!* "I needed to go to a training class, so it wasn't a real break."

"It's just that... well... it's a bad time of year."

It was always a bad time of year. "I understand. I have so many days owing to me though. HR advised..."

"I will speak to Tamara." Sheldon rolled his shoulders, looking stressed. "Couldn't you postpone for two weeks?"

It was always the same. The only time he ever signed off on her leave was when Shaun intervened, which wasn't happening this time. He went on before she could answer.

"Just think about it. It would be a great help to me." Funny how he was making it sound like she actually had a choice in the matter.

She wanted to scream the word 'no.' To tell him to go to hell. Erin had always bent over backwards for the Jones family. Her whole life had changed after meeting Shaun. Things would have been so different if they hadn't gotten together. They'd be different now too if he hadn't—She pushed that thought aside. "Okay," she conceded. "I'll think about it." What choice did she have?

Sheldon's face lit up. "I'm sure that nephew of mine will come to his senses really soon. You're a catch, Erin. A real catch."

"Thank you," she mumbled. This was definitely a conversation she didn't want to have. Certainly not with her boss, who just happened to be her fiancé... her ex fiancé's uncle. She needed to stop thinking of Shaun as hers. He wasn't! They might never get back together.

"I just put a pile of orders on your desk." He pointed to her already cluttered work surface. Hinting that she should hop to it and right then.

"My lunch hour started a few minutes ago." She forced a smile.

"They're urgent." He widened his. eyes

"I'm sorry." She shook her head. "I have plans that I can't cancel. I will get it done by the end of business."

"Fine," he groaned, looking hard done by.

Erin turned and walked out, holding back an eye-roll of epic proportions. It was rare for her to take lunch. She normally ate at her desk, working between bites. Yet he was acting like he was doing her a favor by letting her go.

Once she made it to her car, she dug in her purse and

Dragon GUARD

EARTH DRAGONS BOOK 1

CHARLENE HARTNADY

Copyright March © 2019 by Charlene Hartnady
Cover art by Melody Simmons
Edited by KR
Website Simplicity

Proofread by Brigitte Billings (brigittebillings@gmail.com)
Produced in South Africa
charlene.hartnady@gmail.com

Dragon Guard is a work of fiction and characters, events and dialogue found within are of the author's imagination and are not to be construed as real. Any resemblance to actual events or persons, either living or deceased, is purely coincidental.

No part of this book may be reproduced in any form or by any electronic or mechanical means, including information storage and retrieval systems, without written permission from the author, except for the use of brief quotations in a book review.
First Paperback Edition 2019

DEDICATION

To my favorite cat lady.
Alex, this one is for you.

pulled out the burner phone tucked away in the side pocket. There was only one number programed into the device. Erin dialed it.

"Hey," a voice on the other end answered after a couple of rings. "How are you? I'm so looking forward to…"

"I'm postponing the mission."

"What? I thought we had everything all planned out. We were looking forward to seeing you… both of you. To having you join our group."

"Me too," she said. "I'm having trouble getting off work."

"Leave. Pack a bag and walk out. There's nothing keeping you there anymore, is there?"

That made Erin think of Shaun. Was she being silly holding out? Maybe Deborah was right. Maybe she should just walk out. Start over.

"I'd prefer to do this my way," she finally said. "My boss has promised I can take the time I need in two weeks. I've done the training. The prep. I'm ready. Two weeks is all I'm asking for. Unless there's been some news?" She heard a desperate edge to her voice.

"No. It's like she's in the wind."

"That's good though, isn't it?"

'Yeah, no news is good news.

"Two weeks," Erin said.

There was a long pause on the other end of the line. "Okay."

"We'll talk soon."

"Definitely." The line went dead. Erin tucked phone back in her bag, still wondering if she was being stupid. *Shit!* She checked the time. At this rate she was going to be late.

It was Jenna's birthday. Her best friend was celebrating with her family that evening, so it was now or never if she wanted to spend some time with her. *She did!* She didn't have many people in her life. In fact, Jenna was 'it' right then. Her eyes stung, and her chest felt tight. She blinked a few times, holding back tears.

She headed for her car and drove to Java Hut, which was a few blocks up the road. Her phone buzzed with a message as she pulled into a parking space.

Jenna: Be there in one. Please wait for me.

Erin typed back that she would. She couldn't help smiling. Of course she would wait. She would never think of going in without her friend. Jenna had always been like that. She didn't like walking into a place alone. Erin worked hard at being on time for their get-togethers because invariably Jenna would end up sitting in her car until she got there. She'd once waited for almost half an hour for Erin to arrive. It was just a quirk. Jenna had never given any real reason, just that she didn't like going into places alone.

Almost a minute later, Jenna pulled in next to Erin who grinned and waved. They got out of their cars and hugged. "Happy birthday," she said.

"Thank you! Although, this is a birthday I could've done without." They let go of one another. "I'm thirty next year. Did you know that? Thirty!" Jenna widened her eyes. Like it was the worst thing ever. Erin was twenty-eight and single… well, sort of. Lately, she'd heard the ticking of her clock. Especially late at night while the world was sleeping. *Tick. Tock. Tick. Tock.*

Erin pushed her glasses back into place and laughed.

"Of course I know your age. It's just a number though. No biggie."

"You're right." Jenna smiled. "It's just that I'm a year older and still have this bucket list that's a mile long." Jenna gave her an odd look. "Talking about things on bucket lists, I still can't believe you know how to fly a helicopter."

Erin shrugged. "Yeah... well..."

"Don't say it's no biggie because it is. Not many people can say they know how to fly one of those things."

She almost wished she hadn't told Jenna about it, but her friend had asked about the training class she was taking and well, she'd told her. It was a two-day pilot refresher training program. She needed to be prepared. "I haven't flown in years. I didn't want my license to expire, that's all," she mumbled, hoping Jenna would change the subject. Thing was, her friend knew very little about her past. Like the fact that she not only could use a gun but could disassemble one in under ten seconds. She allowed her eyes to drift over the parking lot and stiffened as she caught sight of the white Range Rover a few spaces over. *Surely not?*

"What is it?" Jenna followed her gaze.

"I doubt it's even his." Erin giggled sounding nervous, which she was. She adjusted her glasses and walked a little further into the lot so that she could get a look at the license plate number, and sure as hell... *it was his.*

Her shoulders must have slumped because Jenna said, "Shit! It's him isn't it?"

Erin nodded. "Yes, but that's okay. I don't mind." She pretended not to care. It was no big deal. "I know how much you love Java Hut's frozen coffees and how you'd kill for their double chocolate cake." She forced a smile. "I also love it… as does Shaun."

Jenna made a face. "Okay, so we love it, but—"

"But nothing," Erin interjected. "It's your birthday. I'm out celebrating with you. Let's go have the cake. So what if Shaun's here. We're adults, and besides, we're on good terms." She began walking in the direction of the coffee shop, but Jenna clasped her arm before she could take more than a step.

"Are you sure?"

"Yes." Erin snorted, waving a hand as if it was nothing. It *was* nothing!

"I know how your break-up has affected you. You've cried on my shoulder far too many times over the last two months." Jenna looked worried, she was frowning heavily.

"We're not broken up… I mean we are, but… it's complicated." She sighed.

"I wish you'd just move on." Jenna got that 'schoolmistress' look. "That man doesn't deserve you."

"We're on a break," Erin tried, knowing it would fall on deaf ears. "We're going to get back together soon."

"You know my feelings on this."

"I do." Only too well. "Let's not argue about this. Not on your birthday." If they continued with this conversation, they would argue. Erin took her friend's hand. "Do you want that double chocolate cake or what?"

Jenna looked skeptical for a moment and then nodded. "I do."

"Let's go then." Erin pulled her shoulders back and they headed for Java Hut.

"So how is…" Jenna faltered, then pulled in a sharp breath, putting herself between the door and Erin.

"Actually," her voice had a weird edge to it, "I don't feel like the cake, and the frozen coffee gave me heartburn last time. Let's go for sushi." She spoke quickly. Too quickly. Her smile was wide. A little too wide. "Cake isn't even real food."

"Since when has that ever stopped us? What is it?"

"Nothing!" Jenna took her arm and tried to turn her around. "I feel like sushi. That's all." She sounded too upbeat.

"What's going on?" Erin tried for the last time, being firmer with her tone of voice. "I know you, and I know something is up."

Jenna sighed, stepping to the side. "It looks like Shaun is moving on," she replied. "He's here with another woman."

Erin felt her heart beat faster as she spotted them. Shaun was indeed with another woman. *Oh god!* He was with a stunner of a woman. A younger woman. She was pert and toned and wearing an amazing suit. She was gorgeous.

They were sitting in the booth she and Shaun used to sit at. She felt her heart sink… to be more accurate, it plummeted.

"I'm so sorry," Jenna whispered.

They weren't touching but they were sitting close, facing one another. Shaun was looking at the woman like… like… he had once looked at Erin. Even worse, a sticky cinnamon bun sat untouched between them. Why did it have to be a cinnamon bun? That was *their* thing. Coming to this place was *their* thing and he was here with another woman.

The woman in question laughed at something he said,

and Erin's heart felt like it was pumping blood laced with shards of glass. The tiny splintered kind. The piercing kind. She made a weird noise, quickly clearing her throat to try to cover it up.

"Let's go," her friend urged, using a soft tone.

Shaun glanced up and they locked eyes for a moment. His widened with recognition. Then he smiled and went right back to talking. Just like that. Like she didn't exist. Like the last seven years had never happened.

"I'm so sorry," Jenna whispered again.

"It's not your fault." Erin sniffed, trying not to sound like her heart was being ripped to pieces. "Sushi sounds fantastic." She allowed herself to be turned back towards the parking lot.

"You don't have to pretend with me," Jenna said.

It was her friend's birthday. She wasn't ruining it over Shaun. She'd spent too many hours crying over that man already. She was going to suck it up for Jenna. "Nah! I'm fine. Let's go. I'll follow you. I love sushi. You know that."

"That is true," her friend said as Erin's phone vibrated in her hand. She looked down at the screen.

Shaun: Daniella's a friend from work. Hope you are well xx

"It's a message from Shaun," she explained, showing the text to Jenna.

"You don't believe him, do you?" Her friend sounded sad.

"I don't know." It was the truth. She was so confused right then she didn't know what to do. What to believe. "I want to." Also the truth.

"You shouldn't," Jenna countered. "There was

something between them."

"Let's go to lunch," Erin changed the subject. Jenna had never liked Shaun. That didn't make her the most objective person in this instance. She loved her friend though and didn't want to ruin her birthday by arguing over this again.

One thing was for sure, she needed to take that week off work. Sheldon could fire her if he wanted. There was something important she needed to do. The sense of urgency suddenly grew. Her life was a mess. There were things from her past that needed sorting out. Wrongs that needed righting. She knew that she'd be in a better position to deal with all of this when she came back.

CHAPTER 2

The next day…

King Blaze stepped forward and a hush fell over the large crowd. Males elbowed their friends and comrades, who quickly closed their traps and turned to face the front. The hum of excitement was electric. There was this buzz in the air that caused gooseflesh to rise on his arms.

"Welcome to the hunt!" Blaze yelled.

The crowd erupted. Males growled, snarled and shouted. Many raised a fist or stomped on the ground. Mountain didn't so much as move a muscle. He kept his eyes on the Fire king. This was a time for focus and determination. The noise around him died down almost as soon as it began.

"As is tradition, the human females have a head start," Blaze continued, his voice booming across the sea of males. All four tribes were assembled. "They are out there as we speak." He gestured to the vast wilderness behind them.

Several males hollered or bellowed. Just hearing the words made blood rush through Mountain's veins.

Human.

Female.

Blood pumped harder through his veins. He so badly wanted to win one. Judging by the cat-calls and the general scent of testosterone in the air, he could tell every other red-blooded male felt the same. There had to be hundreds in the crowd around him.

Blaze held up a hand, signaling for silence. Once again, a hush befell the crowd. He was certain that a pin could be heard dropping just then. "I know you've all heard this a good couple of times but please pay attention," Blaze went on. "I need to go through the rules. You will have to remain in your skin for the duration of the hunt, including on the return leg with your newly won female in tow. The only time you may change into your dragon form, is when you are at the base of your lair. Shift, even for a second, before that, and you forfeit your opportunity at mating a female."

A male jostled in next to him, throwing in an elbow. Mountain scowled at the son of a... it was Shale. The male grinned. "What did I miss?" the Earth prince asked. Shale was both his superior and his friend, which could be annoying.

Mountain nodded once in greeting. "Nothing," he mouthed, before looking ahead. He wasn't sure why Shale was even there. The male was the only prince who had partaken in the last few hunts. He should have won a female a long time ago. He'd given away an opportunity, at least one time that Mountain knew of. It was clear, he didn't actually want to take a mate, so why did he keep going through the motions?

"Good, you know how bad my FOMO is," Shale whispered. "That's fear of missing out, in case you didn't know."

"Furthermore," Blaze raised his voice, sending the Earth prince a dirty look, "the Fire dragons may not use their abilities." That elicited grumbles and moans. Largely because the rest of the tribes were still permitted to use their abilities. "You may not use your fire-breathing ability under any circumstances. None of you are permitted to take or use weapons of any kind. Hand-to-hand combat only, and then only if the females are at a safe distance. You need to keep in mind at all times that the safety of the much weaker humans is paramount. No one wants to see a female harmed in any way. Are we in agreement?"

Shouts and yells went through the massive crowd. "Only once a female has been marked with a male's scent can he be considered the victor, and even then, another male may still challenge."

Thankfully, such challenges were rare. Working even more in his favor was the fact that he was a big motherfucker. His mother loved to tell the story of how he was not only the heaviest male born that year, but the heaviest one born that whole century. Only by a few grams, but he still outweighed Obsidian. Hence his name… Mountain. Let any male try to take his hard-won female and he would pulverize them. Mountain felt his chest vibrate as a low growl left him, eliciting another dirty look from the Fire king. This time directed at him. "You may not kill fellow dragons… you may only maim." He narrowed his eyes.

Shale chuckled softly. "You do know he's talking to

you, right?"

Maim… *Bring it the fuck on!* Mountain would tear limbs off of anyone stupid enough to take him on. The male to his right took a step away. At least the fucker knew what was good for him. So far, he had never been able to win a female. This time would be different. He just knew it.

"Your goal is ultimately to claim your female, this will secure your opportunity at convincing her to mate with you."

Claim.

Mountain had to bite back a groan. Hundreds of males squirmed and shuffled at the mere mention of claiming a female. The tension was palpable. The scent of testosterone grew sickening as each and every male in attendance pictured themselves between the soft thighs of a human female. It couldn't be helped.

Claim.

Mountain longed for a human female. Like most males of his species, he was driven to procreate. They were base in many ways, most especially since their numbers were on the decline. It had sent their instincts into overdrive. *Must hunt female. Must claim. Must mate.* These mantras would be going through all of their heads right then. He glanced at Shale. *Most of their heads at any rate.* Shale seemed immune. The drive in him grew and grew with each passing day. Especially since hunts were limited nowadays.

The dragon slayers were fucking with them big time. Sending choppers into their territory, kidnapping humans and dragons left, right and center. Thankfully there had only been one casualty, but as a result, this was the first hunt in a long time. Hence the high emotions.

The high testosterone levels, on the other hand, were

because the stag runs – designed to blow off some steam – hardly ever happened anymore either. This was due to all the extra patrols and added security measures. Extra security meant more work, less time for play. It had been close to eight months since Mountain had been with a female. All of them were feeling it. Even when they did get out, one night wasn't very long. Mountain would sometimes head home in the morning feeling even lonelier than before he went.

A human female of his very own. Someone to warm his bed every night. To bear him young. To talk to. To hold. To cherish.

Yes!

Hell, yes!

"The biggest prize… it isn't to win a female." Blaze shook his head. "It isn't even the claiming of the female… It will be when she allows you to mate her." That was exactly what Mountain had been thinking.

A roar went through the crowd. This time, Mountain roared just as loudly as those around him. How could he not?

"Hold up!" The Fire king was smiling, which was rare. "It's not as easy as you think. Although the females out there," Blaze pointed to the mountains in the distance, "want to be here. Even though they want non-human mates, they still won't be easy to win. Be yourself, but," he seemed to be mulling it over, "you will also need to rein in some of your instincts. Humans are different in many ways. Not as forthcoming. Not as straight down the line. Far more reserved. They like polite males. See to their needs. Get to know them."

"Now that part sounds good." Shale shoulder-bashed

him. "Don't you think?" Many of the males around them spoke in this fashion.

"I'm not talking about rutting." Blaze shook his head. "Human females want more than just compatibility."

Mountain frowned. *What else could they want?*

"Yep," Shale whispered. "They are hard work," he muttered.

"And don't think that they will be swayed by trinkets and gifts either." Blaze shook his head, smiling broadly. Looking completely out of character.

Dragon females wanted attraction and compatibility. That was first and foremost. Secondly, they wanted a male who could provide for them and keep them safe. If a male ticked those boxes, she would generally allow mating and quite quickly as well. There was no long, drawn out courtship. When a male and female were ready, it just happened. Done!

Humans couldn't be too different, could they? He had interacted with them on many occasions. Mountain looked down at himself. At first, they were intimidated by his sheer size and muscle mass. But it wouldn't take long for them to warm to him. He had been called good-looking and impressive. He'd been told he had amazing eyes. To him, they were brown. Nothing much to write home about, but he'd had plenty of females tell him they were gorgeous. He'd been called sexy as well… so it must be true. He could tick that box – at least, he hoped he could.

As far as 'provide and protect'… no problem! Done and done! Tick and tick.

He had this. Mountain might be big, but he was fast and quiet as well. There was no way he was leaving today without a female. Not fucking happening. Also, he vowed to himself, there was no way he was letting his hard-won female leave. Mountain was going to convince her to mate him. He'd do it by any means possible. It was going to happen!

Blaze droned on for a few more minutes. Then the warning bell, to signal that the start of the hunt was near, was rung. He noticed how males moved away from him. They knew better than to get in his way. To get anywhere near him.

Shale was the only one in his immediate vicinity. What the male didn't realize or seem to comprehend, was that as soon as that final bell was rung, they would be deemed equals. Since Shale was his biggest adversary, he was about to be taken out.

Shale said something but Mountain ignored him, hoping the male would take a hint. He felt every muscle rope and tense as he prepared to go into battle.

Three… two… one … the bell rang out. A shrill clanging that was barely audible over the sudden growls and grunts. Males elbowed one another. Others took off at a sprint. Many more fell from blows, or after being tripped.

Shale tried to run but Mountain raised a fisted hand, aiming at the male's face. Just like that… *Crack!* Shale went down like a boulder, landing with a hard thud. Mountain almost felt bad. *Almost!*

As it was, he had no time. Mountain roared as he took off at a run, felling any he came within hitting distance of. Bones broke. Blood spewed. Mountain reveled in the violence, knowing what was to come.

A human female. *Mine!* He roared as he surged forward.

CHAPTER 3

Another large shadow blocked the sun for a moment or two. Erin held her breath, pressing herself against a tree. She stayed completely still. If she could do it, she'd stop her heart from beating, but then she'd be dead and that would defeat the whole purpose of her plan.

What was going on? How had she gotten this so wrong? Maybe it was all a misunderstanding.

Once all seemed clear, she pushed out a soft breath, looking down at her arm. Erin clutched at the bloody wound oozing just above her elbow. It was superficial but a real reminder of what could have happened. Thankfully she'd come fully prepared, or she'd be dead now. A pile of ash.

Erin continued to move, wincing as gravel crunched under her boots. She stood still for a few moments. Nothing stirred. Not even a bird chirped, or an insect scratched. Nothing. *Dammit!* This wasn't good. Was one of them stalking her right then? She swallowed thickly, looking around her. Using all of her senses, trying to pick up something. Anything.

She was being silly, Erin finally decided before continuing, careful not to step on anything else. Dragons had fantastic senses, best she take every precaution.

She hesitated mid-step as the hairs on the back of her neck stood up. Her skin crawled. Adrenaline surged. Everything in her told her to run. There was someone behind her. Someone watching. She willed herself to calm down. She was just on edge, that was all. There was no one there. In a few seconds, she'd feel silly. Both relieved and silly and in equal measure. Erin slowly turned to the side, scanning through the thick undergrowth. Her heart slowed just a smidgen when she saw nothing. When, once again, she heard nothing.

"Is somebody there?" Her voice came out sounding shrill and nervous. Then she turned around completely. Searching through the undergrowth… searching… Erin sucked in a breath as her eyes landed on him. He was huge, with eyes that bored straight through her. She watched as his muscles hardened up, which was something, since they were enormous to begin with.

Her mouth dropped open as she noticed the silver marking on his massive chest. *Shit! Holy freaking shit balls!* It was one of them. In the flesh.

His eyes narrowed in on hers. So, this is how prey felt. Surely this was when her life should flash before her eyes. There was no time for that though. Within three seconds flat, he had her hands pinned above her head against a large tree. *How had he moved so quickly?* "You're that slayer," he snarled. "You're wanted by the dragon shifters. I'm taking you in." His voice was deep and had a gravelly edge. His jaw was clenched tight. His eyes blazed.

Then Erin realized what he had just said and frowned. "No, I'm not. You have it all wrong." It was hard to breathe under his scrutiny. He stared daggers at her. His muscles were even bigger up close. Trying to break free would be futile, so she forced herself to stay calm. To stay completely still.

"Nope, you're her... that female... Alex Bell. I saw your picture, and now, I'm—"

"No, I'm not..." she said forcefully and then looked up at her hands, the ones he was still holding tightly. *Shit!* She was in trouble. He didn't look happy. What the hell was going on? Was this shifter going to try to kill her as well? It seemed she had this whole thing all wrong. There was no other explanation. She needed to prove to this hunk of muscle exactly who she was, or she was in trouble. That much was clear. "Look, I don't have the tattoo. I'm not a slayer. If I was, I would be marked. Alex Bell is marked. I never got that far in my training. I left... I ran away, so no tattoo."

He laughed. "Please, you expect me to believe that?"

"I don't expect you to believe anything... take a look." She gestured to her hands. "See for yourself."

His eyes stayed firmly on hers for a long while. His frown deepening. Erin forced herself to stay still. Not to say anything more. It was up to him. Surely, they would know about the tattoo. They seemed to know a lot about Alex.

Still clasping her wrists, Mountain finally took down her hands and inspected them, front side, underside... left arm and then right. Nothing. She could see his mind working. Could see the shock. He rubbed his thumbs over the surface where the tattoo should be. He looked up at her before rubbing slightly harder. Like he was trying to rub off some concealer. *Yeah! Good luck with that!*

"See. I'm not her. I'm not Alex Bell. In fact, I'm here to see her. I'm trying to find her."

"Bullshit! You look just like her," he growled. "You have to be her. There is no other explanation." He shook his head, frowning hard.

"Yes, there is, I'm her identical twin sister. My name is Page." It felt weird saying her given name after all these years. Weird but good. "My name is Page," she repeated, feeling something ease inside her.

Page.

Page.

Page.

Not Erin.

Page!

She felt almost cleansed. It felt good.

"What?" he growled, drawing her back to the here and the now. "No," he shook his head, "you're just trying to fuck with me."

God! This guy was slow. "I'm not trying to mess with you. Why would I do that?"

"To save your ass." His hands tightened around hers.

"Wait a minute." She shook her head, frowning. "I thought Alex was here on dragon territory, that…"

"Why would we have a slayer here?" He sucked in a breath. "Unless you thought we had captured her. Are you here to attempt a rescue?"

"So," she paused, "you *do* believe I'm not Alex then?" She raised her brows. That was something. It didn't seem like they had Alex though. Where was her sister? What was going on?

"I'm not sure what I believe." He finally let her hands go and she rubbed them to try to get the blood flow back in her hands.

"It was my understanding that Alex was with a shifter – that the two of them are together."

He snorted out a laugh that held no humor. "Okay now that's a load of BS if I ever heard it!" the dragon snapped, his eyes blazing.

"It's true. Alex must have finally realized what our father was all about. She escaped with a shifter. Killed one of the founding house sons to do it too… Good for her." She spoke more to herself than to the dragon. Her sister's ex, Harry, was a dick. A sadistic asshole devoid of a heart. No one deserved to die but he came close.

Leaving Alex all those years ago had been one of the hardest things she'd ever had to do. Her sister had been so under the influence of her father and Harry, convincing her would have been impossible. So, she'd left without her twin. Left without so much as a backward glance. She regretted it at times. Today, was one of those days. "Where are you, Alex?" she muttered, looking up through the gaps in the canopy at the shards of blue sky.

"I think you have it all wrong. You're talking about Beck who was captured and later escaped. He is here on dragon territory. Alex Bell is still number one on our wanted list. He never mentioned anything about a relationship with the slayer. He would never…" The shifter made a face of disgust.

"They escaped together," she insisted. "I have it on good authority that my sister left the organization. I assumed they would come here… together. Whether as friends or more I don't know." She shrugged. "I gave it some time... a cool-off period. I thought by now she would have convinced your kind that she is not a threat." She knew Alex. There was no way her sister would have fallen in line with their father's evil plans once she knew about them. A person couldn't change their fundamental roots and Alex was a good person. "I thought I would find her here." She had been so sure.

"Not a threat? Are you out of your mind? Beck did come back... alone. There is nothing between the slayer and him. He wouldn't go down that road. Would never betray his people like that."

"I don't understand!" she muttered. "I trust my source implicitly. She maintained that Alex was still in the dark about the organization up until recently. I know they definitely escaped together as a team. They had been intimate, so I assumed—"

"My kings would never accept a slayer!" His voice was a deep rasp. "I need to take you in for questioning." His stance was hard. His eyes piercing.

Page pushed out a breath. "Fine! Take me in." She said it like she actually had a choice in the matter, which she clearly didn't. "Hopefully someone will have more information for me. I'm desperate to see Alex. Our father has eyes everywhere... they're searching for her. I hope she's changed her identity. It seems she's on more than one Most Wanted list." By the way that dragon had blasted her helicopter out of the sky earlier, it was kill now, ask questions later. Despite the two-day refresher, she was rusty as hell at flying.

Without thinking about it, she looked down at her arm. Her sister was in grave danger. She burned with the need to help Alex, to see her sister again. Although, she wasn't sure how that was going to be possible. Not now. Page had a feeling she was going to have a hard time convincing the dragons she was one of the good guys.

"Are you hurt?" His eyes filled with concern.

"I'm fine."

"What happened?" He reached for her, but she pulled away. "It's nothing. My arm caught on a branch as I came down."

"Came down from where?" He frowned.

He really was clueless. He obviously wasn't part of the search party currently looking for her. "One of your kind attacked me. Great big dragon came out of nowhere and blew a fireball my way. My chopper went down. I'm not sure how I made it out alive." She groaned. "It was a rental. I'm going to be paying for the rest of my life for it." She should never have paid extra to have her pilot license added to her new identity. "I knew this was a bad idea."

"He must have thought you were the slayer... Alex Bell." He held up a hand. "Just for the record, I'm not convinced you're *not* her."

Page wanted to roll her eyes but held back. She thought about mentioning her glasses but was worried he would say they were fake, which they actually were. If he caught her out, he wouldn't trust her, and she needed to convince him. "My hair is longer." She finally blurted, touching the tip of her blonde ponytail. "Let me show you." She pulled out the elastic band holding her thick mane in place, allowing her hair to tumble down her back. Page even turned, giving him a better view. "My sister's hair is styled, it comes to her shoulder blades. My hair is much longer... almost down to my butt." She was actually way overdue a visit to the hairdresser.

"I see that." His voice was deep and resonating. He didn't sound convinced though. "You are welcome to check it out. Go on," she looked back over her shoulder, "give it a tug. Put your fingers through the strands. I'm not wearing hair extensions… it's real."

"Hair extensions?" He sounded confused. "What are hair extensions?" He let his fingers trail through her hair, from her roots down. Goosebumps lifted on her arms. She ignored her body's reaction. It had been a while since she had been touched in any way.

"Fake hair," she quickly said. "They attach it… somehow. I don't know the ins and outs since I've never had it done. My sister would not have been able to grow her hair this quickly. How recent was the picture taken of her?"

"It's approximately two months old."

"See," she shook her head, "I can't be her." Page turned around. "My hair is too long."

Damn but he still didn't look convinced. "I don't know about the hair. I can't remember the length, only the light coloring. Yours is exactly the same. Your eyes and mouth are identical. A tropical ocean blue and lush full lips." He spoke like he liked what he saw, his eyes dipping down to her mouth, something heating in their depths. *Come on!* She was reading this wrong.

How did she convince him? "What about my boobs?" she finally blurted, feeling completely exasperated. It was the one thing that was slightly different about the two of them. "Mine are somewhat smaller than Alex's. Or should I say… not quite as big, since I've never suffered in that department."

CHAPTER 4

As hard as he tried, he couldn't help it when his gaze moved down to her lush breasts. She wore a pair of faded jeans and one of those long-sleeved shirts. Light grey cotton and snug-fitting. Especially around that section of her anatomy.

His groin tightened when he realized she was wearing a lacy bra. At least, that's what it looked like. He could just make out the outline of her plump nipples.

"Hello." The female waved her hand. "Excuse me… you can stop undressing me with your eyes now."

Then it hit him. *Fuck!* The female was right. He nodded once. "You're not her. I believe you now."

"What? Why do you suddenly believe me?" She put her hands on her hips, thrusting her magnificent chest out even more. By scale but she was beautiful. Beautiful *and* not a slayer. Well, more than likely not. A great combination in his opinion.

"Um…" What were they talking about? *Oh yes!* "Your breasts *are* smaller. Not by much though. They're still very plump." He smiled, realizing he looked a bit goofy, but unable to help himself.

"Unbelievable," she all but growled, looking angry. "You actually recognize that I'm not Alex based on my breasts? I wasn't being completely serious when I said that in the first place."

"You *were* being serious though." He frowned, not understanding what she meant. "Like I said, your... mammary glands are... less big." He was sure to use her words this time, knowing that human females could be touchy about their bodies.

"Excuse me!" She sounded mad. "You can look me in the eyes now." He could hear that she wasn't happy.

Oops! He'd made a rookie human error. No staring at their breasts, no openly scenting them. "Sorry!" He quickly lifted his gaze, meeting her blazing blue irises. Just then, he picked up the sound of wings flapping in the distance. "Quiet!" he growled below his breath. Mountain pushed himself against her, her back was plastered against the large trunk of a nearby tree. Her stunning tits were pushed up firmly against his chest. *Not thinking about that!* He watched her face as it turned stormy. She was preparing to tear him a new one. He pointed up. "Shhhhh," he murmured.

Her eyes widened as understanding filled them. Not ten seconds later a shadow passed overhead. He stayed put as the minutes ticked by. Mountain could scent her floral vanilla scent beneath the smoky smell of fire. He could hear her heart racing. Her breath as it filled and left her lungs. He could feel her heat, yet could still hear the almost silent flapping as the dragon continued to circle. What was wrong with him? He should shift and take her back to his lair. Should call on the dragon above them, right then to assist him. His kings would want to question her. This slayer. No, maybe she wasn't a slayer. She didn't have the mark. Yet, he could feel all of her softness pushed up against him. Mountain strangely believed her when she said she wasn't one of them. She seemed genuinely concerned about her sister. Genuinely shocked that the female wasn't on dragon soil.

Then again, maybe it was his dick talking. He was attracted to Page. She was sexy as fuck. He'd jerked off to that picture of Alex on numerous occasions. That was how he knew about the breast size difference. If that made him a sick fuck, then so be it. Page was quite lovely and now he'd captured her. During a hunt. Captured! *Wait a minute...!*

"Is he gone," Page whispered.

That's when he realized he still had them up against the tree. All of Page's softness against him. Her eyes were wide, she bit down on her lower lip. He could scent fear.

"Sorry!" He stepped away. "I was just making sure, and yes, he's gone."

"Okay... shew!" she exhaled. Then her eyes flashed to his. "Wait just a minute. Why did you hide us? Why didn't you call that dragon over? Turn me in?"

He clenched his jaw. Not sure how to answer. "I don't know." He finally went with the truth. "I should have."

"But you didn't... because you believe me." She smiled. The female... Page, was gorgeous when she was angry, even more gorgeous when she was serious. She was an absolute stunner when she smiled. "Hello!" She narrowed her eyes on him. "What's going through your head? You got this strange look in your eyes."

"I should have turned you in and maybe the next time I will. I haven't decided whether I believe you or not. I'm pretty sure that by the time we get back to my lair, I'll have a better idea of what to do with you though."

"Of whether or not you're going to help me, you mean?"

"Help you with what?"

"To get back home so that I can find my sister." Page worried her lip, looking nervous.

Mountain had something else in mind. Something else entirely but helping her find her sister would be a given as well. Only so that he could turn Alex in, of course, which might be problematic. It was a bridge he would cross when he got to it. There were several hoops that needed jumping through first.

Then her shoulders slumped. "I just realized that you guys are really fast… especially when you shift into your dragon form. I mean, you can fly for goodness sake. That doesn't give me much of a chance to sway your decision. We'll be back at your lair in no time."

"I'm not shifting. You will have plenty of time."

She frowned. "You're not? Why not? I don't understand…"

"If I shift, we'll be spotted. We're hiking back. I want a chance to get to know you. To decide if I trust you. It's ultimately up to you though. Either I shift and get you back pronto but then you're on your own when you get there, or we hike back. You will then have to prove to me that you're not a slayer." He wasn't being completely honest by offering her a choice. In reality, there was no choice. He would need to take it slow to make absolutely sure she wasn't being followed or concealing a tracker. To be sure she was telling the truth, really. There was no way he was taking her back to his lair until he was sure about her. The lives of his people were at stake. That's what it boiled down to in the end. If she felt like it was her choice, life would be a whole lot easier.

She cocked her head. "It would be strictly to decide whether you trust me, you don't have an ulterior motive? Or do you?"

He shouldn't have ogled her breasts like that. "Relax!" he snorted. "I need to know whether or not I should help you. I must be completely off my rocker because I'm inclined to believe you." He winced when she clapped her hands and smiled broadly.

"So, you'll explain everything to your people and let me go, so that I can find Alex?" Her eyes darkened with anxiety as she said her sister's name.

"Don't get too excited yet. Just because I want to trust you and am inclined to believe you, doesn't mean that I'm convinced yet."

"I understand why you would feel that way. I just wish I could convince you now! I need to get to the bottom of this. I'm not Alex. I don't have a tattoo." She touched her hand. "I'm not part of the organization. I need to find my sister. I don't have time to mess around. Plus, I'm not sure how spending time with me will change your mind either way."

Mountain paid special attention while she spoke. Her heartrate remained even, as did her breathing. Page showed no telltale signs of lying. Humans were fairly easy to read. It didn't work all of the time, but he could generally tell if a person was telling the truth or not. Their heartrate would go up, their scent would change. They'd very often fidget or not look you in the eyes while they spoke. Then again, she might be a very good actress. Mountain wasn't taking any chances. He hoped Page was telling the truth but only time would tell. He'd get to the bottom of this.

"It's how it's got to be. If we hike back, I'll be in a better position to help you. It's as simple as that."

"Is that because you'll trust me?"

"There's more to it." *Maybe. Hopefully.*

"How so?" she narrowed her eyes.

"That's all you need to know for now. I guess you'll have to trust me on that note. If we go back quickly, you'll have a hard time convincing my people that you're not a threat. I won't be able to protect you because I don't know you." Mountain knew this female wouldn't like his real plan. He would tell her about it at the last possible moment. "It'll take two or three days to make it back." It would take twenty-four hours tops but he needed more time with this female, to be sure she wasn't the enemy. "You have exactly that long to convince me."

"What will happen if I can't?"

"I'll hand you over for questioning. One way or another we'll get to the bottom of why you are here."

"I already told you. You and your people can question me all you like." Her eyes blazed and her little hands curled into fists.

"If you're telling the truth, I'll know soon enough. I promise I'll protect you and I also promise to help you find Alex." Most likely so he could turn the female in. He struggled to believe that Alex wasn't a slayer. Page was mistaken.

"She's a good person." The female looked at him with

defiance in her eyes.

Mountain shook his head. "We may need to agree to disagree on that one." The female in question had kidnapped people. Had them tortured and had even shot more than one of the water dragon males. *Good person? Like hell!*

"She is… I swear. Our father—"

Mountain put up a hand. "We will have plenty of time for talking. Trust me… I want to hear all about it. Right now though, you need to take off your clothes."

She blinked in surprise. "Did you say take off my clothes? I thought I heard you say that, but… but… that can't be—"

Mountain nodded. "Yes, that's exactly what I said. Strip! Do it now, please."

CHAPTER 5

Page felt like asking him the same question again. She felt like checking to see if she had heard correctly because surely it wasn't the case. He wasn't really asking her to undress, *was he?*

"Um… I normally expect dinner and a little dancing before I get naked for a guy. At the very least, knowing his name would be a good start."

The big bear of a man shook his head. "I'm sorry. How rude of me. I'm Mountain." He held out his hand.

"Mountain… right." She took his much bigger hand, marveling at how warm it was. How rough and calloused his skin felt. He really was a mountain. His name suited him. He looked like a linebacker. Tall, wide shoulders and packed with muscle. A gorgeous silver tattoo glinted on his wide chest. He wore blue cotton pants and nothing else. Not even shoes. His eyes were a stunning golden chestnut color. His jaw was lightly stubbled. Now that she'd gotten over her initial shock, she realized he was attractive. Very different to Shaun, who was average height and build with perfectly styled hair. Her fiancé – ex-fiancé – she needed to keep reminding herself of that fact. Why was it so darned hard to remember? Thankfully, given the situation, no fresh pain flared, she was too busy trying to talk her way out of—

Mountain gave her hand a squeeze, bringing her back from her own musings. He then let it go. "I want to find us somewhere safe to hole up for a few hours." He looked up into the canopy above them. "At this rate, someone is bound to spot us." His jaw clenched. "You would be taken immediately." He looked like he didn't like the idea. "We need to hurry this up. Take your clothing off and we can be on our way." He shuffled his feet, folding and unfolding his arms.

"No way!" She shook her head. "You're nuts. Why do I have to undress?"

"Your sister wore a tracking device. Thankfully it malfunctioned because it could have led the slayers straight to one of our lairs. I can't trust you yet, even if I wanted to."

"A tracking device? You seriously think I'm wearing a tracking device?" If Page dug deep, she could understand his concern. Still, making her strip seemed a bit drastic.

"I'm sorry, Page, but I have to be careful. We're about to hike to my lair. I could lead you straight to my people. Hand you the location of my lair on a silver platter. Your father is bad news. The slayers would come and annihilate us. It's not a risk I'm willing to take." He kept explaining himself, looking slightly flustered. "If it helps any, shifters are used to nudity. It's natural for us." He shrugged like it was no big deal.

"It's not natural to humans," she muttered, more to

herself than to him.

"I see you're not wearing any jewelry…" His gaze moved from one hand to the other, zoning in on the finger where, up until recently, an engagement ring had sat. He cleared his throat, his eyes moving to her watch. "That has to stay here." He pointed to her watch.

"It's my Fitbit."

"I don't care. It has to come off… I'm sorry. I don't want to argue. This is how it has to be. It's that or I'm alerting the next dragon who comes overhead, and we're taking you in."

"Fine," she huffed. Shaun had given it to her. Maybe it was better if she took the thing off. She began to unbuckle it, pausing, what if they got back together though? He wouldn't be happy if he found out she'd lost it.

"Page," the shifter said for a second time.

"Um… sorry… yes." She shook her head, trying to snap out of it. She wasn't used to being called that again after all these years.

"We need to hurry," Mountain urged.

"Sorry, yes, I understand." She looked back down at her watch.

Screw Shaun!

He had broken off their engagement. He was the one who had moved out. He was the one having coffee with someone else. Not the other way around. She yanked the watch off her arm and put it down on the ground. "Are you sure this is completely necessary?"

"I'm afraid so. Hand me each item of clothing so that I can check them. I also need to be sure that you don't have one attached to your body somewhere." He looked up at the branches overhead, his eyes narrowing.

"Is it another one?" she whispered.

He put a finger to his lips, gesturing to the tree. She quickly pushed herself against the bark, hugging her arms around the trunk. Mountain came in behind her, pressing his huge body against her. He was hot, making her think that dragon shifters ran at warmer temperatures than humans.

She shut her eyes as the shadow loomed overhead. Page felt his breathing pick up. Hers did as well as adrenaline surged. Was this the same creature from just before? Did he suspect that they were hiding? She prayed hard that they wouldn't be discovered. The last thing Page wanted was to have to prove herself to the dragon species, who would see her as a huge threat. Not two hours ago, a dragon had fire-bombed her from the sky. It was a miracle she had even survived. No, she needed to do what this dragon said. At least for now. She didn't have much of a choice.

Mountain stiffened. There was a cracking noise. At least, if she strained her ears she picked it up. No, it was gone. Had she been hearing things? Wait! Was that...? Holy shit! It was! Yes, there it was again, an almost silent footfall. She realized that she couldn't hear the flapping noise from before. Was that him? The dragon?

She concentrated on breathing slower, on staying calm. Page hadn't been to church in a while, but she found herself praying. It seemed to take forever. Mountain hardly breathed. He didn't move.

Finally... finally... there was the sound of flapping again and then silence.

Mountain finally stepped away from her. He was frowning heavily. "Let's go!" he whispered.

"Was that…?"

He nodded. "That was close."

She pushed out a breath, her eyes feeling wide. "Too close."

"Let's go… we've got to move before he comes back."

"How the hell did he miss us?"

"We'll talk later." His eyes were blazing.

"What happened to stripping?" she whispered back. *Why had she even asked that?* It seemed like he was letting her off the hook, so why make a big deal of it?

"We need to get to safety before we are discovered." She noticed that he still spoke under his breath and that his eyes kept straying to the canopy above.

"Do you think that dragon knows we're here?" she whispered.

"I think he suspects that something is here. There is a good chance it was the same one from earlier. Let's get moving. You need to be quiet. I suggest that we don't talk for the time being."

She nodded once.

He hunched down in front of her, facing away from her.

"What are you doing?" Page whispered.

"I'm making it easier for you to get on my back."

"I can walk you know."

"I'm going to run, and you won't be able to keep up. Also, I'll be a lot quieter than you." He said it all as a matter of fact. There was zero sign of an overinflated ego.

Okie dokie then! Page climbed up on his back, locking her ankles around his middle.

Mountain hoisted her higher, holding onto her thighs to keep her in place. Thank god she was holding onto his shoulders, or she might have fallen back as he took off, taking big, powerful strides. Her mouth fell open at the sheer speed. She quickly closed it though when a bug almost flew in it. Page held on for dear life. She realized something else, he *was* quiet. She couldn't hear his feet land. There was no crunching of gravel or snapping of twigs. Nothing!

And boy did he have stamina. On and on they went until her arms and fingers hurt from holding on. Until her thighs hurt from clenching around his waist, but he continued like it was nothing. He didn't huff or puff. He didn't slow down at all. On and on and on, until sometime later, Page wasn't sure how long – at least forty minutes but most likely closer to an hour – he stopped and put her down. It was so abrupt that she staggered, and he had to grab her arm to steady her or she might have fallen.

They had cleared the forest and had reached a rocky, hilly outcrop. "You stay here." Still no heavy breathing from the exertion. She knew all about shifters from all her teachings growing up but seeing one up close like this was something else.

She nodded. "Okay."

"I mean it. Do not move. Do not make a sound… no matter what happens." He touched a nearby tree. "Can you climb?"

She looked at him like he was nuts. "Um… why would I need to climb?"

He touched a low branch. "I want you up here and then there," he pointed to a higher branch, "if need be. Move quickly. You need to do as I say, Page."

She nodded. "Okay. I'll climb if I have to."

"Good. I won't be more than a minute." He sprinted

over the rocky outcrop, disappearing behind a large boulder.

A great roar sounded from somewhere inside the hill. At least, it sounded like it was coming from inside. It was muffled. Whoever had made that noise was big and pissed. She wondered if it had been Mountain or—Another roar sounded. This time it was deeper, even more terrifying.

Screw waiting! Her heart pounded as she hoisted herself onto the first branch, getting ready to climb higher. There was a crash followed by a snarl.

Her eyes almost popped out of her skull when a huge grizzly bear lumbered from behind the boulder. Page swallowed thickly, watching as the beast ran off. It didn't even look her way. Bears didn't have tails, but if this one had had one, it would be firmly between its legs right then.

Mountain came out from behind the boulder, he made his way to where she was perched on the branch. Like it was nothing. Like he hadn't just scared off a bear. He offered her a hand.

"That was seriously impressive but... um... a better warning next time would be nice." She smiled at him, taking his hand and leaping from the branch. "So, you knew he was in there?" she asked.

"Yeah." Mountain nodded, letting her hand go. "I could scent her."

"Her?" She raised her brows. "That was a girl bear?"

"That was a pregnant female. That's why I went easy on her, I didn't want to harm the cub in any way. We needed to borrow her cave for the night."

"You could tell all that?"

Mountain nodded once. "Yep, I could scent it." He touched a finger to his nose.

"I suppose you could. I mean, I knew about your superior senses but that's crazy. You could scent her pregnancy?"

"I could scent that her hormones are subtly different, also, I could hear the cub's heartbeat."

"That's amazing. What can you tell about me?" She looked down at herself.

He didn't answer for a few beats. "Not much. You scent too much of smoke. It messes with my abilities to pick up on subtle notes."

She pushed out a breath. "Interesting I must say, now I feel bad we chased that bear away. Since she is preggers." Page looked in the direction the bear had just run off in.

"We'll leave in the morning. That female will hang around and come right back once we're gone. She'll be absolutely fine."

"Oh shit! She'll hang around?" Page widened her eyes. "What if she comes back sooner?"

Mountain chuckled. "She won't come back while I'm here. We'll build a fire just to be sure. It can get cold out here in the mountains at night."

"Okay... you sure she won't come back?"

"It'll be just fine. I'm here, I'll keep you safe."

She *did* feel safe with Mountain. How could she not? He was as solid as a rock. Back home, when she'd still been living with Shaun, Page had always been the one to check if there was a noise at night, or to take out uninvited spiders since she would never let Shaun kill them. Even spiders deserved a chance. It had never been the other way around. She watched as Mountain searched the open sky above them. "We'd better get under cover."

She nodded, following him to the boulder. They circled

around it. The entrance was smaller than she thought it would be. Page had to bend down to get into it. That bear must have just fit. Mountain had to crouch down and bend his knees as he negotiated the entrance.

Once you were in though, it opened up into a fairly large space, at least it seemed pretty big since she couldn't see all the way in, or all the way to the ceiling. It smelled musty… like bear, she guessed, since she didn't know what bears smelled like.

"Here," he took her hand in his much bigger one and squeezed lightly, "come over here and sit down." He steered her to a smooth rock.

"I'll be back in a little while."

He tried to let her hand go but she held on tight. "Wait! You're not leaving me." She heard the panic in her own voice and felt like an idiot, but it wasn't something she could control.

She heard him pull in a breath. "I'm going to fetch some firewood. I won't go far."

"You'll keep an eye out for that grizzly?"

He chuckled. "I thought you were a badass slayer."

"I'm not! That's what I've been trying to tell you." More panic.

"Sit tight! I won't go far. You'll be okay… I swear." He gave her hand another squeeze before pulling away.

She listened as he moved away, crouching through the opening and disappearing. Page was too afraid to move in case she stubbed her toe. She kept her eyes on the opening of the cave where light streamed in. Tried not to think about what could be lurking in the back of the cave. The part she couldn't see into. She tried hard to hold back the panic she felt whenever she felt trapped in the dark. Like it was closing in. The space becoming smaller and smaller. "I'm in a big cave." Her voice was shrill. "A big, big cave."

The air also seemed too thin. Like the dark sucked away the oxygen, making it hard to breathe. "There is air." She pulled in a deep breath. "I can breathe." She sucked in another breath, keeping her eyes on the light. "It's fine. I'm fine."

A few minutes later, Mountain returned with an armful of logs. Page instantly felt better, now that she wasn't alone. He put the wood down, some distance from where she was sitting. "Told you I'd be quick." She could hear he was smiling, even though she couldn't see him properly.

"I appreciate it. I guess I'm not a huge fan of the dark." She hugged herself. "It's a fear most kids outgrow. I wasn't one of them." She waited for him to mock her, like Shaun had teased her in the past. It never came.

"I'll fix that in just a minute…" She could hear him tinkering with the firewood, obviously building a fire. Then there was a scratching noise. Like he was rubbing sticks together.

"What are you doing over there?" she asked.

"I just need a spark." His voice was strained.

"Can't you just breathe fire?"

Mountain didn't answer. Obviously not, since he kept on with the rubbing.

"Do you need some help?" she tried.

Mountain made a noise that told her he didn't and carried on with what he was doing. She saw a flicker of light and heard him blowing. The kindling he held flared, illuminating his face. He put the burning tinder down and added a couple of twigs, which quickly caught fire. It wasn't long before they had a little blaze going. "That'll keep the grizzly away for sure." He smiled, making himself comfortable next to the fire. "I will fetch us more supplies in a couple of hours once things calm down out there." He gestured to the opening of the cave.

Page's mouth was feeling dry and it wouldn't be long before she started getting hungry. He must be feeling the same but there was nothing to be done about it. Page nodded. "Okay."

She moved in closer, sitting on a flat rock. Page held her hands out to the now crackling fire.

"Why is it that you're afraid of the dark?" he asked, perfectly serious.

She shrugged.

He kept his eyes on her for a while longer. "You don't know, or you would prefer not to talk about it?"

"I'd prefer not to talk about it." Page had never told anybody the real reason. The only person who knew was Alex.

He nodded once, seeming satisfied with her answer, even though it didn't reveal anything.

"Why is it that your sister, Alex Bell, is a slayer, your father is one as well, but you are not?"

"Straight to it?" She raised her brows.

"There is no time like the present. It's not like we have anything better to do right now."

She couldn't argue with that. Page wanted him to believe her. She needed help. "For the record, my sister *isn't* a slayer. We need to get that straight right from the start. Does she work for the organization? No, not anymore. She used to but not in that capacity."

He didn't say anything.

"It is my understanding that she is no longer with the organization. I happen to trust my source, who has eyes and ears on the inside. Like I told you, Alex escaped with a dragon shifter. He took her with him of his own free will. In fact, she helped him escape. Even if she was still working for my father, it *wouldn't* be as a slayer."

"I'm not convinced of that, but I am listening." Mountain was frowning.

"Fair enough. As to why I'm not still with the organization... it's a long story but I'll give you the condensed version." She sucked in a deep breath. Page decided to tell him everything. No holding back. It was the only way.

"I'm listening." He nodded. She could just make out his features, which were focused on her. He leaned forward slightly, resting his arms on his thighs.

"I was never a 'daddy's girl'... not like Alex. My sister could do no wrong and Alex worshiped the ground my father walked on. At least until..." She looked down.

"Until?" the shifter prompted.

"Until he realized she was never going to be the bloodthirsty slayer he needed her to be. He hoped she would be. I told you," she looked into Mountain's eyes, "Alex is inherently good. She's kind, couldn't hurt a fly. She tried hard to be everything he wanted. She studied day and night, practiced harder than anyone else I knew. Then one day we were required to take down a deer on a hunting expedition. She couldn't do it. She told everyone she missed the shot. Thing is, Alex didn't miss." Page clutched her hands together on her lap, looking deep into the fire. Watching as the flames licked. "She never missed."

"What happened after she said she missed?"

"The bastard beat her. He... he was... *is* a despicable human being. I already suspected there was more to what was going on, but that day was the tipping point for me. After that, our father became really mean, and not just to me. He lashed out at Alex too, all the time."

"Too? He hurt you as well?" His jaw tightened. Every muscle seemed to bulge and rope. Mountain looked angry. He didn't know her, so she was probably misreading his reaction in the dim light.

"Yes," she whispered. "He is an evil son of a bitch."

"So, your father is an asshole. He hurt you and your sister." Mountain had this murderous look in his eyes. "Is that why you left the family business? You said you suspected more, did you find something out?"

"Yes. It pissed me off when he hurt Alex. It made me so angry watching her still trying to please him. In fact, she worked that much harder after he hurt her, and it made me sick! You need to understand that we were raised to believe that shifters were evil."

He flinched, narrowing his eyes. "That's rich."

"We were told that you guys, the dragons, were the vilest of the lot. That you had plans to retaliate against the humans for all we did to you. We were told you were pissed at our forefathers. That you swore revenge. You were plotting and planning a war against the humans, and that the ground would run red with our blood."

"Why would we start a war with the humans?"

"We almost drove you to the point of extinction, and so you were coming back for revenge. You weren't going to take prisoners. Your plans were to wipe us all out as a species, every man, woman and child."

Mountain's eyes narrowed. "That's crazy!" He clenched his jaw. "We have nothing against the humans, it's the slayers we hate."

"I know that now. Back then, it was different. Although there were holes in the stories we were told, we still initially believed them. When you're brainwashed into believing something from birth, you kind of end up believing in it, even when doubt creeps in."

"You found something out though? Something that made you change your mind?"

She nodded. "I had two close friends growing up. Deborah and Reggie. We would sometimes chat about our doubts... the little inconsistencies we noticed. I was the one to first bring them up a few weeks after our father beat Alex. I couldn't keep quiet anymore. I was shocked when Deborah and Reggie agreed with me that things didn't make sense." She smiled. "After that, we talked often. Alex used to get so mad if she overheard us. She'd stick her fingers in her ears and threaten to tell on us. As we got older, she'd yell at us and storm out, again, threatening to mention it to daddy. Of course, she never did."

"What kinds of things caused you to doubt?"

"We were always being taught attack strategies. Very little defense. Then there were the best torture methods to extract information. We were supposed to be readying to defend the human race against you and yet, it seemed like the opposite was true. It wasn't about being ready but more like rallying the troops. Winning others to our cause. There was never anything concrete, but we suspected."

Mountain nodded. "Something or someone tipped you off."

"My friend Debs was something of a wild child. During our first year in college…" She pulled in a breath. "You need to keep in mind that many of our classes were conducted in-house. All the children of the founding families attended. From weapons training to martial arts and everything in-between. Our martial arts instructor was a young ex-marine that Debs got her claws into. They ended up having a full-blown sneaky relationship. There was lots of pillow talk. He told her some stuff. The more they slept together, the more he told her of the real plans the founding families were cooking up. It all fell into place. We realized their sick agenda. It was worse than we could ever imagine. Every time there was a dragon-spotting – not that it happened often – someone would be sent to gather information. There are many families that belong to the organization. It has people everywhere, in government, high-powered judges, CEOs in major organizations… you name it. Eyes and ears everywhere. Every lead is followed. The many resources used to their fullest. The plan was – and I'm sure still is – to find where you are holed up. Find your lairs, your mines—"

His mouth pulled tight for a moment.

"What? They know about your mines. You know that don't you?"

When he didn't say anything, she went on. "Their ultimate goal is to find you and to kill you all. Every last one of you. Then to take your riches… which are believed to be vast. Gold, diamonds… blood money." She mumbled the last more to herself, remembering the shock. The horror at finding all of this out. They suspected, but they never imagined the magnitude of the evil.

"You believed the ex-marine?"

Page nodded. "Yes, he boasted to Deborah about how rich he was going to be. There was no reason for him to lie. She pretended to be taken with the whole thing. It all made sense. The weaponry that was being purchased. The bombs... the truckloads of silver. We were being trained for war, to attack, to kill... The problem was, I had no evidence, just the ramblings of a guy who hadn't even been born into the organization. I believed, even if others wouldn't. All I knew was that I couldn't stay. I couldn't live a lie. I couldn't keep working for an organization that was planning such large-scale murder. To speak up would have meant death though."

"Your own father wouldn't have... killed you? Surely not?"

He stopped talking when she smiled. "Angelo Bell would have ended me. He still will if he ever gets the chance. It doesn't matter that I am his daughter... in fact, he hates me so much more because I betrayed him. I betrayed the family and the organization. He would kill me himself. I have no doubt my father would have me murdered without so much as blinking."

"Bastard," Mountain spat.

"We had to get out. I tried to tell Alex... I didn't blurt it or anything. I skirted around the subject. I hinted, but she wouldn't hear of it. I had nothing concrete. In the end we left. Reggie told his girlfriend and the four of us ran."

"Where did you go? How was it that you weren't found?"

"We split up, bought fake ID's. I stayed in touch with Debbie over the years. I have a burner phone I change out from time to time. Use it for the odd call to find out what's happening. It's how I found out about Alex. I am thinking about meeting up with Debs again once I find my sister. I might even join their cause she and some others formed against the slayers"

"Might?" Mountain kept his eyes on her.

"It would mean leaving my whole life behind." She shrugged. "I don't know if I'm ready to do that." She wouldn't be able to see Jenna again.

Mountain nodded once, accepting her answer. "What of the male you escaped with?"

"I have no idea where Reggie and his girlfriend are… how they are. They fell off the face off the earth, which was clever of them. Less chance they'll be found out. I also cut all contact with Alex. I didn't want to put her in a compromising situation. One where she would want to stay loyal to our father while trying to protect me."

"How long ago was that?"

"Almost ten years ago. Just before my eighteenth birthday. The day they swear you in… the day you get your tattoo." She touched her unblemished hand.

"What did you do? How did you survive?"

"Thankfully Deb had her own account. Her own money. She was given huge allowances and didn't always spend them all. We cleaned out her account. She was kind enough to split the money. It was enough to keep us going for a few weeks. For us to buy new identities after going our separate ways. We didn't want to know each other's new names… in case… it was safer that way."

"You were seventeen?" Mountain looked shocked.

She nodded. "I celebrated my eighteenth birthday alone. I moved around a lot at first. I was so afraid of being caught. I dyed my hair brown and cut it short. I wore glasses even though I didn't need them. I worked as a waitress, or a cleaner, whatever odd jobs I could find to stay afloat. Then I met Shaun."

Mountain narrowed his eyes and clenched his jaw for a moment. He didn't say anything though.

She tried to play with her ring, remembering too late that it was no longer there. "Shaun used to come into the coffee shop every day. He'd order a cappuccino and a cinnamon bun. He'd always sit in my section and we got to talking. Even after it came time to move, I stayed. Then we started dating. A few months later, I moved in with him. He got me a job as an admin clerk at his uncle's stationary shop. I've since been promoted a few times. It was only after meeting him that I felt safe enough to stop running and hiding."

"Wait a minute... your reaction earlier when I called you by your name... you haven't been going by Page, have you? You said you acquired a new identity."

She nodded. "Yes, I got a new identity and therefore nope... I haven't been Page Bell for years. I'm now known as Erin Janet Blithe. I no longer dye my hair, but I still wear glasses." She touched the frame. "Even though I don't need them. I guess some habits die hard."

"It sounds like you have had it rough." There was a flicker of something in his eyes. Distrust. He still didn't completely believe her.

"That, or I'm trying to get you to feel sorry for me."

"Are you?"

"Only time will tell, I guess," she answered in the only way she could. She'd been honest, telling him more than she'd told anyone in a very long time. Despite him not completely believing her, it felt good.

CHAPTER 6

That evening…

Page sat up, sucking in a breath. It was hard to orientate herself. Her neck felt stiff. What had woken her up? Why—? Her heart galloped when she realized how dark it was. She pushed her glasses into place and widened her eyes. Sucking in another sharp breath, she looked around her.

"It's only me," Mountain said. She could hear the gravel crunch beneath his feet. She could barely make out his outline.

Sparks flew as he threw a log onto the fire, followed by a second one. She heard him blowing, the embers igniting. It was enough to show him hunkering down over the fire, trying to breathe life back into the blaze.

She sighed, feeling the adrenaline leave her system.

Before long, flames began to lick, more gathered. After a minute or two, Mountain added two more logs to the now small blaze.

"Is that a…?" She leaned forward, trying to make out what was lying next to him. It was big and it was dead. She caught the coppery scent of blood, now that she knew it was there.

"It's our supper. It's a deer," he added. "Please tell me that you're not squeamish."

"No, I'm not! I had torture down as one of my subjects in school, remember? I've hunted… I've killed."

Mountain nodded. "Good, because you will need to eat if you are to maintain your strength for the trip back."

"You said it's going to take a couple of days."

He nodded, reaching over to where he had put the deer carcass down. "Here." He handed her a piece of what looked like bark. It was big and curled in on itself. "Careful," he warned.

She gasped as water sloshed over the edge. "Oh! Thanks." She eagerly drank from the makeshift vessel, placing the container on the rock next to her to finish later. Thankful that the worst of her thirst had been quenched.

"Let's get some meat on the fire," Mountain announced.

As it turned out, the meat was delicious. They cooked extra to eat for breakfast. By the time they had finished their meal, she found herself yawning again.

"Get some rest," Mountain advised. "We are leaving at dawn."

"Okay." She watched him lay down on the other side, his back to the fire. Page followed suit and lay down. It wasn't very comfortable. The ground was hard and cold. Despite yawning regularly, it took a long time to fall asleep. She woke often, trying to find a more comfortable position. She heard Mountain put logs on the fire from time to time, so she was never afraid or cold. That was something, at least.

After one of the longest nights she had ever had, Mountain sat up. "Did you sleep okay?" he asked.

"How did you know that I was awake?"

"I can hear it. Your heartbeat is too fast, as is your breathing."

She smiled. "Then you'll know I've had better nights."

He chuckled. "Sorry about—"

"I'm not complaining though. At least we were warm and dry." She stretched, trying to get rid of some of the stiffness in her neck.

"And safe," he said, handing her some of the leftover deer.

"Yep, there's that too." She took the meat from him. They ate in silence for a while. "So," she finally blurted. "What is it that you do? I mean, dragons have duties… jobs too, don't they?"

Mountain smiled. "Yes, we do. I am in charge."

"In charge?" She waited but he didn't say anything more. "In charge of what?"

He shrugged. "Of training, if I really think about it."

"Oh, interesting. What is it that you train?" It was funny, she didn't see Mountain as being a teacher. It didn't compute.

"Defense… mostly." He smiled.

"Oh… so not training as in academics? Training as in… how to kick butt?"

His smiled broadened. "There is a whole lot more to it than that, but yes, essentially I train how to kick slayer butt."

"Well," she pushed out a breath, "all I can say is that I'm glad I'm not a slayer then, because I'm sure you're really good at kicking ass."

Mountain chuckled. He nodded once. "I am indeed." He suddenly turned serious, his eyes on her.

"What is it?" She frowned.

He widened his eyes. "About kicking slayer ass and about you *not* being a slayer. I need to check for that tracker now." He had the good grace to look sheepish. "We can't go any further until I'm a hundred percent sure you're not carrying one."

"I'm not! I swear, there is no tracker," she insisted, knowing full well that she was wasting her breath.

Mountain didn't say anything, he just looked at her.

"Fine!" she huffed, pulling her shirt over her head as she stood up. "Let's get it over with then."

Mountain also rose to his feet, moving quickly and gracefully for such a big guy. His eyes stayed on hers as she handed the garment to him. It was chilly in the cave, the cold air hit her skin. Thankfully it was fairly dim as well. He hopefully wouldn't see her discomfort. She also hoped that he couldn't see through her lacy bra... then again, he was a shifter. He had superior senses. *Not going there!* It was her own fault for wearing such a sexy set. Cute, matching underwear had always been one of her things. Shaun didn't like her wearing sexy numbers. He preferred cotton, so she'd forgone wearing what she wanted because of him. The first thing she had done when he'd asked for her ring back was to go and buy a whole drawer full of sexy things, including the set she was wearing.

She held back another sigh as she unclasped the top button on her jeans and pulled down the zipper. Page glanced at Mountain, who was scrutinizing her shirt. He sniffed at it and felt along the seams with the tips of his fingers.

She wanted to laugh at the absurdity of the whole thing, and yet she couldn't, this was far too embarrassing. Page couldn't blame him for being cautious. If the tables were turned, she might just be doing the same, expecting the same of him.

Page toed off her sneakers, pulling off her socks and stuffing them in her shoes. He put her shirt down on a nearby rock, folding it first. *How nice of him!* Then he held out his hands and took the shoes while she pulled down and stepped out of her jeans. Her cheeks heated. *'He's a shifter and nudity is normal,'* she told herself. Her g-string was white lace, same as the bra. If she looked down, she would be able to see her landing strip right through the thing. If she could see it, then... *Oh god!* Her cheeks blazed. Hopefully, he didn't look too hard.

"I'm sorry about this," he mumbled, kind of glancing her way. He didn't look like he was enjoying himself. That was something at least.

"I'm sure you are." She didn't sound sarcastic at all. Much.

He must have picked up on it because he went on to apologize again. "I really am... sorry that is." He stopped his investigation of her socks and looked her in the eyes. The poor guy looked like he meant it. "I saw that indentation on your finger... that means that you are more than likely mated. I completely understand that this is even more difficult for you, as you have promised to—"

"No!" She waved a hand, shaking her head. "I'm not married. I'm not even engaged. I mean I was, up until not so long ago, but I'm not anymore, so you can relax!"

His shoulders visibly loosened.

"It doesn't make this any easier, you know. I might not... have someone in my life right now... but this is still difficult," she said, handing him her jeans. His eyes dipped down for a moment, quickly flashing up to meet hers once more. If it weren't for the situation, she'd find his obvious discomfort funny. Problem was, she was more uncomfortable than him. Way more embarrassed.

"I'm sorry," he mumbled.

"You keep saying that. You don't have to. I don't like having to take my clothing off, but I understand." She could see he was avoiding looking at her, not in that way at any rate. He wasn't being perverted and gawking at her in any way, which was something. She supposed.

"That's not why I'm apologizing." He picked up her jeans and began his search of those. "I'm going to need your coverings as well."

"Coverings? What do you—?" She looked down. By now the only things she was wearing were her underwear. *Surely not!* "Oh no...!" she began. "Hell freaking no! Don't even..." She hugged herself, trying to cover up. Not that he was looking. It was the thought of going completely naked... like the day she was born... only she was a grown woman. Her chest heaved as a touch of panic set in.

Mountain felt along the seams of her jeans. "I have to. There is no other option. I can't let you go, and I won't take you with me otherwise." He looked up at her, again, his eyes staying on hers. "I have seen naked females before. Most of them were humans."

"Oh, well that makes it all ok then."

"I'm glad you agree." He looked back down at her

jeans, continuing his inspection.

"I was being sarcastic."

"Oh!" He looked pained for a few seconds. Mountain shrugged. "There is nothing I can do. I have no choice here."

"Let me guess, seeing me naked is going to be agony for you."

He frowned. "No, it will... Wait a minute, you're being sarcastic again. Very funny." He sounded deadpan. Maybe he was catching on?

"It's not funny at all. Not in the slightest. How would you feel if I told you to take all your clothes off? In fact, I'll only take my clothes off if you take yours off, and I insist as well." She folded her arms. Feeling like an idiot immediately after the words left her mouth. What was it he had said earlier? Something along the lines of shifters not having a problem with nudity?

Mountain shrugged once. Before she could stop him, or say anything more, he reached down and tugged down his pants. Half a second later they were pooling around his ankles and he was stepping out of them.

She'd only ever seen one guy naked. Page was five foot six. Shaun was around a quarter of an inch shorter, although he would never admit it. Not for the almost seven years they had been together at any rate. He wasn't the biggest man. Not in any aspect. Not that she had much to go on since – well yeah – he had been 'it.'

Her mouth fell open. A soft gasp left her lips. Her whole body went cold and then quickly heated up a whole lot. Like someone lit a match next to an open flame with the gas turned up. She might not have much to go on, but she had a sneaky suspicion if she did, that this would be impressive. In fact, she knew without a doubt that he was remarkable. Jaw droppingly, 'make your head spin' gorgeous.

Page had a feeling you could line up a hundred guys and none of them would hold a candle to this shifter. Heck, you could bring in a room full of marines and they'd have a hard time competing.

His hips were as narrow as his shoulders were broad. It was safe to say he was big all over. *All over!* From his tree trunk biceps to his—She gulped, taking in his man-part. His *penis* – she whispered the word, even inside her own head. *Damn!*

Mountain may have been discrete when it came to gawking at her, but there was nothing discreet about how she was eyeballing him right then. She knew she was doing it, and yet she couldn't get herself to stop. She pushed her glasses more securely onto her face. His... penis... was both long and thick. Very long and very thick. He'd made it sound like he'd been with human women before. She wondered if sex had hurt them. It wasn't just his actual member that was big but his balls too. They were— Mountain covered himself with his hand. His very large, shovel-sized hand. It was only then that the trance was broken, and she was actually able to lift her gaze back to his.

Her cheeks heated up a whole lot more, they must have been the color of beetroots by then.

His expression remained impassive for a few more seconds before he frowned. "Have you never seen a male naked?" He cocked his head, glancing down at her hand for a second. "I thought you were to be mated and that," he shrugged, "that you must have seen a male without clothing, but maybe I have it wrong." He raised his brows in question.

"I have… I um… have seen a guy naked." She rubbed a hand over her face, she sounded like a bumbling idiot.

"Just none like me." He half-smiled.

"Only one guy," she blurted. "And no, he wasn't anything like you." She shook her head slowly, like she was in a daze.

"What?" His frown deepened. "You've only ever seen one male naked? You are no longer a young female. I assumed—"

"Gee thanks!"

"I mean, you are mature… in your prime."

"I think you're trying to compliment me, but I'm not sure." She smiled. "Yes, I've had the same boyfriend for quite a number of years. Seven to be exact."

"Years? Seven whole years without mating?" Mountain sounded shocked. "You spent years dating the male? Forgive me, dragon shifters don't like wasting that much time. It seems strange to a shifter. That is all. Please do not take offense."

"None taken. Probably wise not to date that long." She thought of all that time she'd wasted on Shaun.

He let his hand drop to his side and her eyes moved right back to his… his member. "I'm sorry, it's just that you are different. Very different! You say you," she cleared her throat, "you've been with… had human girlfriends." She forced her gaze back up to his.

"No, I've never had a girlfriend. I've never dated either."

"Oh, I just assumed when you said you've seen naked women that—"

"I've fucked quite a number of human females." So

evenly delivered it had her mouth falling open again.

Page cleared her throat. "Oh." Her voice came out all croaky. Only because she felt this tug of need between her legs. Her clit did this little pulsing thing.

Mountain turned around. Holy hell but his ass was gorgeous. Meaty gluts she could see herself squeezing. *Where had that come from?* She forced herself to look away, but he bent over to pick up a log and then threw it on the fire. *Wow! Just wow!* He was really attractive.

He frowned when he caught her staring. She really needed to get a grip. "Maybe you should put your pants back on," she blurted. Not liking the brain fog.

He openly sniffed the air. "I can scent your arousal."

"I'm not aroused!" she half-yelled. Then she stopped herself from saying anything more and shrugged. He would know in a hot second if she denied it. He'd be able to scent it. "It's... it's not..."

"I can see this whole thing is making you *very* uncomfortable."

She bit back a nervous giggle and nodded instead. "Just a tad. It's not what you think by the way. I just haven't seen a naked guy in a while. Maybe I... I am reacting somewhat to that. Don't let it give you a big head or anything because it's... not like that." It wasn't like she was interested in him. She was there trying to find her sister. This was serious business.

He widened his eyes for a moment. "I am working hard to control my own arousal, so you need not worry about a big head." His eyes dipped back down to her cleavage, but he quickly averted his gaze.

Working.

Hard.

Arousal.

It didn't help to know that he was also aroused too. Mountain picked up his pants and put them back on. *Thank god!* She could breathe again. "Please take off your coverings. I will make this as quick and as painless as possible."

Oh god! Could she do this? Did she have a choice? "Shaun – my ex – is the only guy who's ever seen me naked." Her voice was soft and apprehensive.

"He is one very lucky male." Mountain ran a hand through his hair. "I don't know what else to suggest. I need to be sure. You wanted me to undress and I was happy to oblige. If there is something else I can do to make this more bearable, you only have to say the word and I will happily make it happen. If there was any other way." He looked uncomfortable.

"Um… you can close your eyes… maybe turn around. I'll hand you the items and you can check them. You don't need to actually see me naked, do you?"

Mountain looked down at his feet before locking eyes with her. "I'm afraid I do. I need to check you… every inch of you. Not just your clothing. Tracking devices are small and easy to conceal."

Page squeezed her eyes shut while his words sunk in. *Crap!* This was worse than she thought. Then she pushed out a heavy breath. "Well, we may as well get it over with. My sister is out there somewhere. One of your kind knows where she is… I hope. I need to find out one way or another. If it means having to take my clothes off so that you can start to trust me, then so be it." She reached behind her back and unhooked her bra. Page covered her breasts with one arm and her hand, while using the other to hand him the garment.

CHAPTER 7

Mountain took the scrap of fabric from the female, working hard to quell his need. He had been able to see all of her just fine through the flimsy lace. From the fur between her thighs to the tight nubs on her lush breasts. Not that he had allowed himself to openly look. In fact, he'd tried hard not to see any of it. He felt bad for the female. It wasn't like he had a choice here though.

His groin began to tighten just thinking about her soft skin, her lush thighs. Mountain looked at the far wall, taking in air through his mouth… tasting her fragrance on his tongue. She was sweet and decadent. Deliciously human. He couldn't scent another male on her, so her story about not being attached to someone else must be true.

Good!

Aside from being attracted to her, he liked her. He had a feeling he was going to like her a whole lot more as he got to know her. He just needed to keep a level head. Page might be a slayer. He doubted it, but he needed to be sure

– very fucking sure – before anything more happened.

As with the rest of her clothing, he sniffed at the covering, allowing the delicate fabric to slip through his fingers as he felt for a tracker. The garment was soft and scented strongly of her. Mountain was especially careful around the clasps and the little fake diamond at the front. These would be ideal locations to conceal a tiny tracker.

Nothing.

Good!

"Now for the bottom covering… your G-string." He was sure to keep his eyes trained on hers.

She bit down on her bottom lip for a moment or two. Her cheeks reddened up some more. Mountain felt like the biggest jerk alive. He wished there was some way he could make this up to her. Wished he didn't have to put her through this, but it would be rash of him to trust her right off the bat.

Page leaned down, her arm still covering her breasts but not doing a great job because of how lush they were. If he really looked, he'd see their rounded globes peeking out below her forearm. Their plump cleavage spilling over the top. He didn't look though. He forced his gaze elsewhere. It was the right thing to do.

Mountain felt his Adam's apple work as he took the slip of lace. He kept his eyes averted for the time being. He needed to make this as easy on her as possible.

Just as with all of her other clothing, he let his fingers work over the garment, feeling for something hard and out of place. Feeling—*Fuck… wet!* The seam of her panties was soaking wet.

His cock took note. Mountain had to work hard to keep from becoming completely and solidly aroused. As it was, he could feel blood begin to rush south. *Shit!* He didn't want to scare her. It took him a few long moments to compose himself.

"Are you okay?" Her voice was high-pitched. "You look upset."

"I'm fine." His own voice was a thick rasp.

"You don't sound fine, in fact you sound angry. You look angry. Every one of your muscles is bunched."

Mountain cleared his throat. He *was* scaring her. He really needed to pull himself together. "I swear, I'm absolutely fine. I feel bad, that's all. Don't take this the wrong way." He brought the slip of lace to his nose and inhaled.

Fuck!

Pussy… hot, sweet, wet pussy. It made his mouth water. Made him want to groan and sniff again. He needed to look past the scent of what was nestled between her legs. This would be the ideal place to hide a tracker from a shifter male. He tried again, this time ignoring the delicious scent of aroused female, seeking only plastic, circuit breaker, electronics. He got nothing. Just her. Lots more of her. It had been so long since he'd savored a female. Too damned long. Especially one as delectable as this. She was a heady mix of gorgeous, vulnerable and defiant.

Mountain swallowed down his need. He looked down at the floor for a moment, waiting for his vision to return to normal. His eyes had turned slitted, more dragon than human in that moment. The need to fuck invading every pore, every sinew and muscle. By now he was sporting a semi but only because he forced himself to think about shitty things. A full-blown erection would scare the shit out of Page. Of that he was sure.

He looked back up at her, noting how she tried to hide herself from him. It made him feel worse. "How do you want to do this?" Mountain looked around the cave.

"What do you mean?"

"I need to check you… thoroughly."

"Thoroughly? What does that mean?" She shook her head. "If you need to check me, then check. Just get it over with."

"Would you prefer to lie down or to stay standing?"

"Standing!" she answered without hesitation. "My boyfriend and I aren't really broken up… not really." She looked nervous, her eyes darting to him and then to the floor and then back to him.

"I thought you said—"

She squeezed her eyes shut for a second or two. "We're no longer engaged and we're kind of together but not." She bit her bottom lip.

"I don't understand, either you're with someone or you aren't. I don't mind that you're telling me all this but at the same time, you need to know that there is no relevance." He felt his heart sink. He'd been so sure that this hunt wasn't a total loss. Especially when she had said she was no longer promised to this male. That maybe he stood a chance at winning this female even if she hadn't come here to find a mate. "It doesn't matter either way… I still need to check for a tracker."

"I don't know why I told you. Maybe because you're easy to talk to and you're about to see me naked. I think I might be nervous… see I'm babbling." She laughed. "I did feel something just now when you spoke about… When you said…"

"When I spoke of fucking."

The scent of sweet arousal met his nostrils and he had to fight the urge not to sniff.

"Yeah, that. Maybe I feel guilty or... god! I don't know. Thing is, Shaun and I are on a break. We're not actually broken up. Well, we are but..." She groaned. "It's complicated. I'm not sure why I didn't tell you that when you asked me earlier." This female was attracted to him. He could see it, smell it, feel it.

Good!

She was telling him all this because it scared her.

"I don't know what 'being on a break' means." He shook his head, frowning.

"A break. It's exactly how it sounds. We're still together, well sort of. We're just taking a break from one another." She kept one arm hooked around her breasts and her hand firmly over her sex. He kept his eyes on hers.

"How long is this break supposed to last?" It sounded like a bunch of bullshit. He decided to hear her out though before commenting.

Page shrugged. "I don't know... a couple of months." Her eyes welled with tears. "He never specified."

Shit! "Look, I'm sorry." Mountain shook his head. He could sense her sadness, which told him that she most likely wasn't faking, but this could be an act to keep him from checking her for a tracker. "I find the whole thing quite bizarre. Seven years of dating?" He made a face, feeling confused about the whole thing.

"We were engaged for two and a half of those seven years though."

"Even worse!" He wanted to bite his tongue when her eyes got all hazy and her face crumpled a little. "Look, if I was with a female… someone like you… if I was serious, even seven weeks would be a long time. Seven years is ridiculous. An engagement? There'd be no engagement. I'd pop the question and mate you the same day." He clapped his hands together to prove a point. "Done!"

"You're a shifter though. You do things differently."

Mountain shook his head. "Not so different. Not really! Why does he need a break? I'm still not sure I understand what that even is."

She shrugged. "I'm not sure I understand it either. He said he needs some time to find himself before we get married. That he needs some space." She shrugged. "I couldn't say no to that. He told me to give him a little bit of time… asked me to wait for him in the meanwhile."

"It sounds like he wants an opportunity to fuck around before settling down with you," Mountain blurted. "If you're okay with it, then I guess it's fine."

Page burst out crying. She looked down at the floor, tears streaming down her cheeks. She made this little sobbing noise. Her shoulders shook.

Mountain felt like putting his foot in his mouth and chewing it off at the ankle. He felt like a dick. What the hell was wrong with him? Why did he blurt that out? Maybe because it was true, but still, he could have been more diplomatic. "Shit! I'm sorry! I don't have any tact. Here," he handed her shirt back, "cover yourself. Let's chat about this first. We can worry about the stupid tracker later."

"No, you're right." She shook her head. "What you are saying makes sense." She took the shirt, holding it over herself but not putting it on. She took off her glasses and used the back of her hand to wipe her eyes. "You're absolutely right. I saw him with another woman yesterday. They were having coffee together. He sent me a text afterward to tell me she was just a friend from work, but..." She rolled her eyes, which were filling with tears all over again. She blinked and swallowed and blinked some more.

"But you don't believe him?" Mountain finished the sentence when Page left it hanging.

She shook her head. "I don't think he's sleeping with her. They didn't look like they were intimate." Her tears came faster. "I'm sorry. I guess I haven't had much of a chance to think this whole thing through. Then again, maybe I have but I didn't want to think about it." She sniffed. "Maybe he *does* need space. Maybe they *are* just friends." She bit down on her lip. "I'm really confused about it. I still don't know why I'm telling you all of this. I don't even know you."

"You needed to get it out. You must have been looking for an objective opinion. It's clearly been on your mind."

She put her glasses back on. "It has. Maybe I also needed you to know that I'm taken." Her eyes widened. "Not because of anything except for the fact... well, I'm naked. This doesn't feel right for that reason. It—"

"I'm checking you for a tracker."

"I might be attracted to you... just a little and I feel guilty about it. What about Shaun? He asked me to wait."

Shaun was a douchebag. "Actually, you're on a break which means you're fair game. Not that I'm about to take advantage. I wouldn't do that."

Page nodded. He could see that she wanted to say something because she opened and closed her mouth a couple of times, seeming to think better of it.

Mountain didn't want to see her cry again, but he didn't like that this jerk was dicking her around. "I might not be human, but I can tell you that if he wanted to be with you, he would be with you. There was be no need for a break. If he wanted to mate you… marry… whatever the right term is, he would have done so. He would never have fucked around for so long. This asshole Shaun is jerking you around, keeping you on a string so that he can reel you back in once he's had his fill of other females. What pisses me off the most is that he's told you to wait for him." Mountain raised his brows. "Unbelievable," he muttered.

"Look, we are technically broken up, but," she shrugged, "he knows I would never jerk him around… not if I imagined us getting back together in the back of my mind – and I do." She pulled in a breath. "I guess I ultimately do," she spoke softly, "even now, even after seeing him with that Daniella woman. I guess it's still there, that hope… that…" She clenched her teeth. "Screw it and screw Shaun! I realize this is strictly clinical and that you have to do this. I'm not going to feel guilty about it. You're an attractive guy but that doesn't mean anything either."

It sure as shit did.

Page put her glasses back on and dropped the t-shirt. She opened her arms, giving him a clear view of her body. "This isn't cheating. It's… something you have to do… are being forced to do."

Forced.

Guilt flooded him. She was right, this was no hardship. In fact, the opposite was true. Mountain was sure to keep his eyes on hers. It wasn't easy, considering how fucking gorgeous she was but he did it anyway. His dick had already decided that there was nothing clinical about this. "I'm not going to apologize to you again, even though I want to. All I'm going to say is that this Shaun bozo is a stupid fuck!"

Page snorted out a giggle. "That's sweet."

"It's the truth. You're too nice for him."

"You think I'm nice, but you're still going to check me for a tracker?"

"It's a formality. I really want to trust you, Page. I'm sure I can but I still have to do this. I'm sure I don't need to tell you how evil your father is... how evil the whole lot of them are."

"You don't, that's why I ultimately understand. That's why I'm standing here naked in front of a stranger. Please can you get this over with."

"Of course." He glanced down at all of her nakedness and almost groaned loudly. Then quickly looked back up. "I will try to think respectful thoughts."

She smiled. "Thank you."

"I'm attracted to you as well... I'm not sorry about that. I need you to know that I am and that it can't be helped. It's probably not something I should admit but hey, there it is."

"It's fine!" Her smile broadened. "It's good to know I'm still attractive to the opposite sex."

"Not just attractive... off the damned charts hot. You're way out of that jerk's league," he growled the last, but only because he meant it.

She snickered. "How can you say that? You've never even seen him."

"I don't have to see him. I'm looking at you." His voice

had a husky edge.

She licked her lips. "That's sweet."

"I guess I'd better get to it. It's pretty cold in here." Her nipples were tight… a delicate pink and hard as fucking nails… hard like his dick was getting right about then. He walked up to her. "Can I run my fingers through your hair, touch your scalp?"

"Sure. Don't be touching anything else though." She laughed at her own joke, sounding nervous.

"I wouldn't dream of it." Her hair was soft and silky. It still smelled of smoke but not in an unpleasant way. He placed the tips of his fingers against her scalp and rubbed across her flesh using firm, slow movements. Careful not to pull her hair.

Her breathing hitched and she closed her eyes. "Wow!" she murmured, her voice sounding husky. "That feels really good." Her voice had an edge to it.

He tried to ignore her comments but when she moaned it shot straight to his balls. If this was all it took to please her, she'd been hard fucking done by. Mountain thought about those same shitty things from earlier and worked his way across her scalp, as quickly and efficiently, as possible. He looked down her slender neck and along her long, elegant back.

Her ass was delectable. He forced his eyes off of it, looking down the backs of her thighs.

Mountain pulled in a deep breath, silently begging his cock to behave as he moved around to her front. "Please raise your arms."

Clinical.

Professional.

Page did as he instructed, and he looked under her

armpits. "You can hide a tracking device just about anywhere," he explained. Hoping she would continue to be understanding. He couldn't be too sure. The lives of his people were at stake, he reminded himself for the hundredth time. Damn this was getting more difficult by the second.

"I'm sorry to have to ask you this." *Fuck, but this was awkward.* "Please can you lift your breasts, I need to see underneath them." He winced as he said the last.

"Oh god!" She squeezed her eyes shut. "Do you really think I'm hiding something under my boobs? Really?"

Mountain tried hard not to stare at her perfect as fuck tits. Big and soft with large plump nipples. Pink was his favorite color, hands down. "Um… no… I doubt it very much but…"

"Yeah, yeah, you have to be sure."

"Yep, I do." He felt like an asshole. No better than her dickwad boyfriend — make that, ex-boyfriend. The turd had asked for the break and Mountain was stepping up. Not right then, not this very second, but he was stepping the fuck up all the same.

She sighed, taking a full mound in each of her hands and gently lifted.

Shit!

Shit!

Oh fuck!

He was getting hard. His balls felt achy. They felt big, and blue and sore.

He watched her throat work and reminded himself of what a dick he was. Her gaze was on the ceiling above. Her cheeks were a bright red. "I guess I wouldn't pass the pencil test anymore." She made that sound like it was a bad thing, which made him frown. "Shaun often mentioned how gravity was a bitch when he saw me naked." She pushed out a quick laugh. "He would often say that more than a handful was too much. Maybe he was right. I wouldn't have to lift them if they weren't a bit droopy. I guess it's the price you pay for having a decent set of boobies." She giggled again, sounding sad and lost and very nervous. *Fuck!*

Anger pounded through him. "Your ex-knob obviously has tiny hands. By your reaction earlier I'd say he suffers from that problem in general."

Her lips twitched, her eyes flashed to his for a moment before moving back to the ceiling.

"I know I probably shouldn't mention it, under the circumstances, but you have stunning breasts, Page. Really plump… that's a good thing!" He was shocked to hear how deep and animated his voice had become. He really meant it though and was pissed off at her ex for putting her down like that. "They are very soft looking, which again, is a *very* good thing. It sounds as if that Shaun male didn't appreciate you."

"I wasn't fishing for compliments but thank you. I was starting to consider having them made smaller."

Mountain gasped. "No! Please don't ever do that… it would be a crying shame."

Page laughed. "I won't! I don't know what made me think it."

"He did!" Mountain growled and then grit his teeth. "That male got inside your head and… It doesn't matter." She didn't want his advice, but he couldn't help himself. "I would recommend that you never get back with a jerk like that. You definitely should disregard anything your ex said to you."

"He's not technically my ex. I agreed to wait." She shrugged, looking like she didn't really believe herself.

"Yes, he is your ex," Mountain countered.

"We're not technically broken up. Well... not really."

"Yeah, you are. You gave the ring back, didn't you?" Her ex had really gotten into her head and in a bad way. "That fucker moved out and was making moves on another female."

"Yes." She nodded. "He moved out of our apartment. We aren't seeing each other at the moment."

"Is he allowed to see other people? I don't mean just for coffee?"

"I know what you mean." Her eyes clouded. "Technically, yes, he is. We're on a break, so he can, but he specifically asked me to wait for him." She frowned, looking sad. "Why would he do that if he planned on fooling around?" Her eyes were big and blue and innocent. This female was no slayer. *Forget it!*

"You..." Mountain forced himself to zip his lips. *Shit!* He didn't want to hurt her. "You don't want to hear what I have to say."

"What is it? I want to know."

"Nothing! As you said, we hardly know each other. If you want to hold out for Shaun, you need to do what's right for you. You need to do what you think is best." He shrugged. "You don't need my opinion. I already gave it to you earlier."

She pushed out a heavy breath. "I told you all of this because the break-up feels off. His need for space feels wrong. Running into him yesterday with that woman... felt really off. He was eating a cinnamon bun. They both were. Drinking coffees and eating their pastries. That was our thing. That's how our relationship started. It felt... wrong!"

"Trust your gut."

"You think he wants to have his cake and eat it too?" She looked down.

"If by 'cake' you're referring to ..." *Your pussy.* He imagined it would be sweet like berry frosting. "To you, then yes, I think he wants to get between a couple of pairs of thighs while on this break. He would prefer it if you stayed faithful while he fucks around."

She made a face, born from pain. He could see that it hurt her to hear. "You sound very sure." She sniffed back the tears that were threatening to fall.

"I *am* very sure! Human males are wired differently. Shifters become fixated on one female. We are driven to mate. We wouldn't even be able to consider fucking around." Why did it sound like he was trying to sell himself to her? Ridiculous. It was too early for that. Even for a shifter. "Humans are different in that regard. Sometimes I think that fooling around is second nature to your species. It's not just the males of your kind, although they are worse. It is sometimes the females too. You would be shocked how many mated individuals are screwing around."

She pulled in a breath, sounding shocked. "How do you know?"

"I scent it. There are times when the males carry a scent of a female other than the one they are with and vice versa. Or when a mated female tries to talk me into sex. I can scent she is mated, can see the indentation on her finger. It is something we don't understand."

She touched her own finger. "I don't get it either."

"I'm sorry I made you take your clothing off. I hate how this must make you feel. I'm sorry I need to do this next part. So damned sorry, Page. Can I call you Page?"

She smiled hesitantly. "It's been so long since someone called me that. It's nice... to be me again, you know?"

"Yes, I can imagine." He scrubbed a hand over his face. "You're too nice to be a slayer. I don't want to take this further. To do the next check but..." He shook his head. "Thing is, I want to trust you but there's just too much at stake." He doubted very much that she was faking the scent of pain and hurt and anger, but what choice did he have but to move forward? To do what needed to be done.

"I'm naked now, you may as well finish it! I need to prove to you that I'm not a slayer. That I left that all behind me. I need you on my side one hundred and fifty percent."

Mountain felt his jaw tighten. He felt everything tighten. "Are you sure about this? It's just, I have no choice."

"Yes, I'm sure! It will be one more box ticked, right? One step closer to you believing me, helping me because I'm going to need help tracking down Alex. You will help right? You promise?"

"I said I would."

"Fine! Finish it. Let's just do this thing. I'll be fine."

"It would mean checking... everywhere."

She swallowed thickly. "Fine!" She gave a sharp nod of the head, her eyes blazing with determination. "You won't need to... to... touch me though, will you?" She sounded frightened. He hated that!

"No!" he all but snarled. "Definitely not." Calmer. "I

would need to sniff at you, I'd need to get in close but no touching. I should be able to scent – maybe even hear – if you have a hidden device."

"By 'hidden' you mean *inside* me?" she squeaked.

"Yes." Fuck, he was a dick. He almost wanted to find something. It would make him feel better. He looked into her big, blue eyes. No, it wouldn't. He'd get this over with and then he was going to get to work on making Page forget that dickhead of an ex ever existed. He only hoped she didn't hate him when he was forced to turn in her twin sister.

CHAPTER 8

"Oh my god this is crazy!" Her voice was shrill. "If there was any other way." His Adam's apple bobbed as he swallowed hard.

Page wasn't sure why she was insisting on this. It almost seemed like he might give her an out if she pushed hard enough. Maybe she was doing it as some act of defiance to Shaun for turning her life upside down. She was about to let another man see her, not just naked, but totally vulnerable. Was it a kind of *'fuck you'* to the man who had hurt her? Was still hurting her? Was it a way of lashing out?

Page didn't know. She still wasn't sure why she had blurted all of this to him. Maybe because she was very attracted to Mountain. Like more than she should be. Especially in this situation. Then again, adrenaline-fueled situations could lead down paths a person normally wouldn't take. She had needed him to know the real situation, even though she felt attracted to him, that she wasn't actually available. Probably because she ultimately didn't trust herself with him. Was that it?

No!

That was stupid. Although not entirely stupid, since she was attracted to him. A woman would need to have her eyes gouged out not to notice a guy like him. But that wasn't it. Page had needed a sounding board. She needed a male opinion. Quite frankly she'd expected him to tell her she had been worried about nothing. She hadn't expected this reaction. From her best friend, sure. Jenna had never liked Shaun very much. Okay, Jenna didn't like Shaun at all. She maintained that he wasn't good enough for Page. Her friend put up with him for her sake. So, when Jenna had been happy about the break, when she'd told Page her opinion of Shaun, it had been expected.

But from Mountain? From a guy. Someone totally objective. No. She hadn't expected it.

Jenna had always told her that she was too loyal, too trusting. Too kind. Was she? Maybe she was. Was she fooling herself, not facing up to the truth? It was distinctly possible.

"I can see you're having second thoughts." His deep, rich voice snagged her attention, making her eyes snap to his. "Do you need a moment?"

"I don't need a moment." She needed to do this and then they needed to move on. "I think I'll lie down. It'll make it easier for you to… do your thing."

"I'll start with your feet."

She nodded. "I'll lie down over here."

"That's fine." Page noticed how Mountain didn't look. He kept his gaze averted. He was very sweet. Both hot and sweet. A dangerous combination.

Page swallowed hard as she lay down. She didn't bother

trying to cover up anymore. What was the point? He'd already seen her breasts and was about to see more of her than anyone ever had before. Except for maybe her gynecologist, and he didn't really count.

Mountain crouched down next to her legs. "Can I touch your feet?"

"Yes."

He took her closest foot in his hand. She giggled when he felt between her toes. "Are you ticklish?"

"I am," she managed to push out between another laugh.

Then he sniffed at her feet.

"That's weird," she giggled again, feeling his breath against her skin, "and ticklish."

"You really are sensitive."

"Yes, I am." She giggled some more as he checked her other foot. Then his eyes moved up her legs... slowly, slowly. Painstakingly so. *Oh god. Here we go!*

He pushed out a breath. "I don't want to even ask."

"It's fine." Page opened her legs. For every inch that her knees parted, her cheeks heated a little more. "I'll pretend I'm at the gynecologist taking an exam."

"That's where human females go to get their female organs checked?"

"Yes, that's the place."

"I will make this quick." He looked her in the eyes as he moved between her legs. "I am truly sorry. I need you to know that I respect you." His eyes dipped down and his jaw tightened. His frown became an all-out scowl. "Again, I shouldn't say anything, but you have one hell of a pretty pussy."

Holy shit! His dirty way of saying things was a turn on.

She shouldn't be turned on right then. Not even close, but hearing him talk, seeing such a gorgeous man between her legs looking down at her like… like… she was his last supper or something. It made her lower belly clench. Especially when he leaned in. Right in. So close she could feel him.

Feel. Him. There.

His breath was hot. This time, it didn't tickle, even though every nerve-ending caught fire. Even though gooseflesh lifted on what felt like every part of her body.

She moaned when he sniffed at her, feeling appalled at her reaction to him. "I'm sorry," she whispered. Her voice was shaky. "I just… I—"

"You're aroused and shouldn't be ashamed of it." His voice was a deep rasp. Lines marred his forehead. His gaze moved back to between her legs.

"Open a little wider and lift your pelvis. I need to get a good look." He sounded upset.

She put a hand over her face, wishing so hard that the ground would just swallow her whole already. "I've never had anyone… never had anyone so close to… I…" She really needed to shut the hell up. She did as he said, biting down on her lip to keep herself from chattering nervously.

"You and this Shaun male were together for seven years?" He sounded angry.

She nodded. "Yes."

"Please tell me that he… that he gave you pleasure." He sat up.

"Um… we had sex, yes…" She nodded.

He visibly relaxed. "Good."

Page could only think about what Mountain must think of her. All that moaning and he hadn't even touched her.

She had sounded desperate and horny. Maybe because she was turned on and he'd be able to smell it as well. Oh god, she wanted to die from the embarrassment. He sniffed her again and she had bit her tongue to keep from groaning. How could the displacement of air feel good? "He never went down on me though," she finally blurted, feeling like she owed him an explanation for her behavior. Another moan hovered on the tip of her tongue. "He's been my only... Shaun has been it for me all this time and so, I..."

She felt him move away, even though he hadn't been touching her. When she opened her eyes, Mountain's mouth was gaping. Then he tensed his jaw. His eyes blazed. "You are shitting me," he growled. "Please tell me you're joking. You were with a male for all that time and what... nothing? He never went down on you?"

She shook her head.

"Not even once?"

"No! So, it just feels... It's fine! I don't mind that he never did that. It's not important. It can't be that good. It—"

"Your reaction to... that... I didn't even touch you for fuck sakes and look at you..." He looked down at her, his eyes turning feral as they raked her body. "Your nipples are hard. Your heart is racing. Your pussy is as wet as fuck. You're so turned on that you don't know what to do with yourself."

She whimpered, quickly biting down on her lip to stop herself from letting any other wanton noises escape. She was giving him the wrong idea. She was acting so inappropriately. Why had she told him all that?

"You're dying for my tongue to be on you. In you. You would love to cream all over my mouth. Well guess what,

Page you're on a break. I'd love to eat you out… to make you scream my name."

Since when had all the air left the cave? She couldn't breathe. She could hear the air rushing in and out of her lungs. She could see her breasts rising and falling in quick succession, but she still couldn't seem to get any air in. Need ran through her veins. It coursed. It beat. It tore at her. "We can't." She shook her head, pulling herself up on her elbows.

"Yes, we can." Mountain nodded. He still wasn't touching her. His gorgeous eyes bore into hers. His broad, muscular chest heaved. His hands were fisted, making his biceps bulge.

"It would be wrong," she whispered; the excuse held no substance.

"No, it wouldn't."

"We don't even know each other."

Mountain smiled. "We're both adults. We're both single. It would be an orgasm, Page, not a proclamation of undying love."

She wanted to say 'yes.' She burned with the need to just give in. To throw caution to the wind. To take for once. To do something random and wild and selfish, but something held her back.

He shrugged his massive shoulders, a smile toying with edges of his mouth. "I think I may have heard something inside you."

"What?" She tried to register what he was saying. "Heard something?" She frowned.

"A tracker, you're hiding one inside you. Admit it!" The edge of his mouth twitched.

"No," she countered and then realization hit. Page

smiled. "I'm not."

Mountain leaned in, right in, his mouth millimeters away from her, his hot breath hit her, making her gasp in both surprise and need. "Oh yes, I definitely hear something." His deep voice rolled over her, making her want to rock her hips. How would it feel? To have his mouth there? On her? How would it feel?

Could she do this? They were on a break. She technically wasn't cheating even if it felt that way.

Mountain began to pull away. "Maybe I'm mistaken."

"I really want to prove I'm not a slayer," she half yelled. The thought of this stopping, of him stopping... Page needed this. It might be wrong but she needed it so badly. More than just an orgasm, she needed to feel wanted and sexy. Mountain made her feel those things. "Maybe you should check it out. Just to be sure."

"No, I think I was mistaken. I think we should be okay. I trust you."

Mountain was sweet. He was making really sure she felt comfortable with this. "Do the check!" She used a commanding tone.

Mountain gave her a panty-wetting smile. "Are you sure about that?" He narrowed his eyes. "You need to think carefully about this, Page. It would mean putting my hands on you. Not just on you but inside you. At least, if I was to do it right. The check that is."

She bit down on her lip as need coursed through her. It tugged on her clit. It pulled from deep inside her belly.

"Not just my hands but my mouth too... my tongue. I'd have to check you over thoroughly."

Oh god! That sounded good. It sounded amazing. She had this aching feeling between her legs. She'd never felt like this before. "O-okay." She was panting slightly but couldn't help it.

"It would be purely clinical though." He smiled. "Completely professional." He used the same words from earlier. This time the connotation was completely changed.

She smiled back, it must look tense and desperate because that's how she felt. "I'm sure it will be."

"Open your thighs wider."

"O-okay," she stammered again and did as he said. There was a part of her that wanted to put a stop to this. It wasn't right. It wasn't… Then there was another part of her that thought back to Shaun, how he had been leaning towards Daniella. Hanging onto her every word. She thought about his facial expression, his smile… all exactly the same as when he had been with her. Back in the beginning. She thought about the cinnamon bun on the table. That did it.

She threaded her fingers through Mountain's hair as he leaned in, watching him between her legs. Mesmerized. He kept his eyes on her as he closed his mouth over her clit. Page cried out, it sounded like she was in agony. That couldn't be further from the truth though. Pleasure rushed through her, seeming to pool right there where he was licking her out. Using firm strokes of his hot tongue.

Licking.

She groaned deeply, gripping his hair with her hand. It felt like she was disembodied right then, because she couldn't make herself let go of him. In fact, she gripped him a little tighter as he sucked on her clit again.

Sucked.

Her back bowed and she yelled, it was a loud punching

noise that reverberated around the cave. She needed to try to be a little quieter, not sure why exactly anymore, only that there was a good reason. Screw reason, she decided when he sucked on her again.

Good lord but her hips were moving, jerking against his face. He slid his finger inside her. "Oh god!" she yelled. "Oh... oh... oh..." She said it with every thrust inside her.

Thrust.

Her eyes were wide. Her breathing ragged. His mouth stayed firmly on her clit. There was this coiling sensation deep inside her. Page had orgasmed before. Of course she had, but she had a feeling that this would be different. That this would feel different. This feeling inside her was big... like a beast... an angry, snarling crazed animal. The animal wanted out and right then.

His finger thrust deeper, moving quicker. It was touching her in a place that had her whimpering and groaning. His tongue flicked out on her clit and this time when he suckled, the beast was let loose.

There was a moment of calm. Her whole body slackened. Her heart seemed to stop. Everything quietened. Maybe it wouldn't be as intense as she had predicted?

Wrong!

Everything tightened and all at once. Her back came up off the ground. The crazed beast screamed as a rush of blinding pleasure tore through her. It clawed at her, wringing every ounce of ecstasy from her. More and more.

It grew... bigger... stronger... so intense her muscles vibrated, her eyes rolled back... her throat hurt, so deep and guttural was her scream. Page came down slowly, one rung at a time. Her hips stopped jerking against him but settled into a rhythmic rock.

Mountain fingered her more slowly, his tongue laved and lapped at her carefully. Her breathless pants filled the space. He finally eased off and pulled out. Page felt like a boneless heap of flesh. She felt drained and sated. She felt… Wait a minute… she was holding him by the hair, both hands gripping him tightly. It took a few more moments to get her fingers to obey her and to let go of him. One of her legs was over his shoulder, wrapped around him. She untangled herself. "Oh! I'm sorry." Her voice was hoarse. She pushed up her glasses and swallowed. "That was… that was… it was…" She nodded too quickly, probably looking like a mad woman. "Intense," she finally managed. "I liked it… um… More than liked actually. Very much." Why was she still talking?

Mountain licked his lips. *Licked,* dammit. His hair was tousled, thanks to her. All of his muscles bulged. Especially the ones on either side of his neck. In short, he was sexy as hell! "I'm glad I could show you some of what you've been missing out on. I would be happy to show you all of it."

"All of it?" she squeaked.

Mountain raised his brows. "Yep… all of it. If you thought that was good, you haven't seen or felt anything yet."

That was the best orgasm of her life. *The best!* It couldn't get any better, could it?

He clenched his jaw for a moment, breathing out through his nose. "Just say the word and I'll happily oblige. I'd like nothing better than to feel you come. Have that tight pussy clench on the end of my cock while you scream my name."

Her mouth fell open. She blinked a couple of times. *Must look like a fish out of water.* She felt another zing of need. *No!* How could she feel turned on all over again, and so soon after coming like that?

Sex. He was talking about sex. Not just sex but dirty sex. Fucking. There it was again, that pulsing need. That clenching, throbbing ache.

Mountain frowned. "I have a feeling that ex-asshole of yours was dissatisfying in more ways than one."

Shaun.

Shit!

"No." She shook her head. "I can't! We can't!" She looked around them, finding her shirt, which she clutched to her chest. "I'm sorry," she continued, still shaking her head. Where was her bra? Her panties? "That shouldn't have happened. It was… Call it a moment of weakness. It can't happen again."

"You did nothing wrong." Mountain moved away from between her legs and she snapped them shut.

"Oh, I know. We're on a break… we…" She was babbling. "I know I didn't!" She left it at that because she wasn't sure she believed it. Page felt guilty.

"I mean it, Page. We did nothing wrong. *You* did nothing wrong. I meant what I said. Say the word and I would love to do that again. I'd love to give you a whole bunch of orgasms… show you what a real male can do."

Page didn't say anything. Especially since she was on the verge of agreeing.

"We're together for two more days. They could be really fun-filled days." He winked at her. "You wouldn't be able to make as much noise though. We'd be found in a hot minute once we leave this cave." He smiled.

Her cheeks heated all over again. "At least you know for sure that I'm not hiding a tracker," Page blurted, trying to change the subject. She *had* been really loud.

His eyebrows raised. It looked like a challenge. "Do I now?" He grinned at her. God, but he was cute. "We'd better get going," he announced before she could argue. "I'll fetch you some water while you get ready."

"I'm in serious need of a shower… or a bath or something." She looked down at herself, grimacing.

"I'm sorry but there's no time and it's too dangerous out here. Later." Mountain handed her underwear back.

She nodded. "Okay… and thank you. For helping me." She took them from him. "For everything," she added. "I'm sorry I couldn't… that I can't have sex with you. I'm not some kind of tease. If things were different…" Page meant it wholeheartedly. She had a feeling she could fall for a guy like Mountain.

"I offered to give you an orgasm. Not the other way around. There is nothing to apologize for."

"Okay. Let's get going then. The sooner we get back, the sooner I get to find Alex."

His eyes narrowed and his jaw tightened.

CHAPTER 9

Mountain could still taste her on his tongue. He could still remember how her pussy had felt as it clenched around his finger when she'd come... hard.

He felt honored to be the first to put his mouth on her. The first. She'd been with that male for seven years. Years, for fuck sake! What was wrong with human males? Not all of them of course. Some of them were assholes though. Selfish bastards. He'd been with numerous human females, many of those females had experienced shock when he'd brought them to orgasm. He didn't understand it. It wasn't that difficult. All it took was a little effort.

The noises she had made... by scale, he was getting hard just thinking about it.

"Are you okay?" she asked.

"I'm good." He glanced back over his shoulder, to where she was perched on his back.

"It's just you got all tense. I can feel it." She used her hands to squeeze his shoulders. "Maybe we should take a break. You've been running for hours since our last rest."

Oh shit! He came to a stop. "Yes, of course. Are you tired?" He put her down. "I should have thought of your comfort."

She frowned. "My comfort?" She looked at him like he was crazy. "Sure, it takes some effort to hold onto you but you're the one doing the running. You're the one carrying me. If it weren't for you, I think it would take us a week to get back." She smiled.

It made him feel guilty. Truth was, he was taking them further away from the lair, to an area he knew the search party wouldn't be concentrating on. It was too far off the beaten track. By now they would know he was missing. He wondered if they knew that Page had survived the crash. The male who had brought her down would have captured her otherwise. Page aside, they would know he was missing and would be searching for him. He felt guilty but quickly pushed the emotion aside. Sure, his motivation was selfish, but it was also necessary. There was very little chance, at this point, that Page was a slayer, but he needed to be sure. "Let's sit for a while. It *is* getting late. We can make camp for the night. Are you thirsty?"

"A little. You must be dying of thirst though."

"I'm okay." He shrugged. They were deep in the forest under a thick canopy of branches. "I'll get a fire started and then I'll take you to the river to wash and drink."

"Okay. Can I help with anything?" She raised her brows. "I can look for firewood."

"You can sit over there." He gestured to a fallen tree. "How is the wound on your arm?"

"You've carried me most of the day and now you're going to make me sit and watch you work?" She cocked her head, putting her hands on her hips. "Don't misunderstand me, I appreciate it but I'm not some wilting flower."

Mountain hadn't spent any serious length of time with a human female. They were different to dragon females, who loved to be treated like queens. Having their every need seen to.

"I can see that. You are welcome to help." He liked her attitude. He liked her, period.

They both got to work. It didn't take them long to gather what they needed. He put the second armful onto the already large pile. He wanted to keep the fire going all night, aware that she was afraid of the dark. He wondered what had happened to her to make her feel that way.

The female watched him as he got to work making the fire.

"You do that efficiently," she remarked.

He gave a one-shouldered shrug. "I am sometimes required to spend nights away from home."

"I thought you were a trainer."

"Training is a big part of my duties. I believe that in order to be most effective within my role, I need to be out with the males, patrolling our borders." He placed the smaller twigs he had just snapped into smaller pieces next to the kindling. "We sometimes spend several days away from home. As much as I enjoy being in my dragon form, it becomes tedious after a while. Certain comforts are appreciated when in our skins. Liking staying warm and dry, and cooking our food. We're less savage when we are in our human form." He smiled, thinking about Obsidian. "My brother is the exception to that rule. He loves his scales. Even when in human form he grunts more than talks. Females are afraid of him. Underneath all of that is a good male though."

"Oh, you have a brother?"

Mountain nodded. Obsidian had been worrying him of late. Spending too much time in dragon form could make a dragon crazy. It could make them lose sense of logic and reason. "Yes, I do."

"Do you have any other siblings?"

He shook his head. "Nope, it's just Obsidian and me."

"Are you very close?"

"Yes, he is my best friend as well as my birth brother."

"You are frowning. I'd say you look concerned." The female scrutinized him.

"That's very observant. Yes," he nodded, "Obsidian has been withdrawn of late. I'm not sure what's going on with him."

"You should talk to him about it. You're lucky you can talk to him," Page sighed. "I wish I knew where Alex was. All I can say is that she's in danger."

"I'm sure she is an intelligent female." Mountain selected two sticks, placed them on top of the dry moss and began rubbing the one onto the other.

"Yeah, you're right." She watched what he was doing with interest.

He kept it up, moving as quickly as he could. The friction would eventually cause heat and then a spark.

"You're good at that. You're really good with your hands." Her eyes widened for a second and she sucked in a little breath. When he glanced up again, her cheeks were pink.

He scented smoke. Mountain bent down and blew on the kindling. It wasn't long before they had a fire going. "That should hold while we head to the river." He felt sweaty and in desperate need of a bath.

She looked like she wanted to say something but ended up nodding instead. "The river is out in the open. We can't take too long." He doubted anyone would be out there, but he couldn't be completely sure.

"I've always loved swimming."

"The water is very cold, so I doubt you'll want to stay in for long."

Her eyes brightened up. "Great! So it will be lovely and refreshing. I can't wait to get clean. I stink." She sniffed at her hair and then made a face of disgust. "I smell like smoke and other things. Gross things."

Mountain thought she smelled really good. Beneath the sweat and grime – hiding under the layer of smoke – was pure female. Delicious human. He wasn't going to think about that right then though, or he'd need more than a cold bath to cure him.

"Come this way." He took her by the hand. "It isn't far. I can carry you if..." He caught her look, which told him not to go there. "But I know you are more than capable."

He helped her over a boulder and then another rocky section. He also held branches, so that she could pass freely. It wasn't long and they were at the deep river. It was wider through this section, so it didn't flow as hard as in other parts of the river. The banks were heavily pebbled.

"Wow!" Page breathed the word more than said it. "That's beautiful. The water is the most incredible blue."

"Like your eyes," he blurted. It was true though, her eyes were the same gorgeous color.

"Thank you." She smiled, letting his hand go.

He needed to calm the fuck down. Page wasn't ready

yet. She still believed that there was hope at a relationship with her ex. She was on the rebound.

She pushed her hands into her jeans pockets. "So, who's going in first? I don't mind waiting. I can wait over there on the other side of those bushes." She pointed.

"Um… we need to go in together. Taking turns would mean doubling the risk of being seen."

Her eyes moved to the open skies, now turning beautiful shades of red, orange and purple. "Surely if we're really quick we could take turns?"

"We have already seen each other naked. I had my mouth on your pussy—"

Page gasped, putting a hand over her face. She pulled in a breath. "You're right! I'm being silly. We're adults. Just because that happened once, doesn't mean it'll happen again. We're responsible and in full control of ourselves. What happened this morning is firmly in the past. What's done is done!"

Mountain had to stop himself from grinning. It sounded like she was trying to talk herself into it, which meant that she *did* want more. It meant that she didn't trust herself to be naked with him. Especially if he was naked too.

"Alright then," he pulled his pants down, stepping out of them, "I take it you won't mind if I wash these." He held up the garment. "I'll need to hang them up to dry for the night."

"The night?" Her voice had a strange edge. "As in, the whole night?"

"I mean, seeing that we're adults and in full control. I agree what happened is in the past, it's done! Doesn't mean there'll be a repeat."

"No repeat. Nope!" She shook her head too vigorously, looking somewhere above his head. Trying very hard not to look at his cock.

"You should wash your clothing as well. I will make us a nice bed using moss and dry—" For whatever reason he was enjoying watching her squirm.

"No!" she half-yelled. "I can't sleep with you. Definitely not if we're naked."

Her overreaction was music to his ears. The thought clearly terrified her. "We can use body heat from one another to stay warm. Don't you want clean clothing to wear?"

"I do, but I'll survive." She had a panicked look.

Good!

This female didn't trust herself with him. He wished her ex didn't exist, or that, at the very least, they were properly broken up. If so, he was sure they'd have a chance at something. This whole 'break' thing was a farce. He only wished she could see it.

"Suit yourself. Get undressed and let's wash up. I will keep my eyes averted and concentrate on the job at hand."

She nodded once. "Sounds like a plan. I'll do the same."

"Stay nearby in case an undercurrent hits, or…"

"A grizzly decides to come for a drink."

"Or that." He kept his eyes on the river. From the corner of his eye, he could see her moving. Probably undressing.

"Okay, I'm ready." Her voice sounded strained. She was probably a bit chilly. There was snow on the mountains. The water was going to be icy. Just what he needed right then. It was hell spending time with a female he couldn't touch. Shouldn't touch, even though he wanted to.

Mountain headed for the river. Page stayed at his side, slightly behind him. He meant it, he wasn't going to look. He was going to respect her privacy. They walked over the pebbles, which made a clattering noise.

"It's best just to get it over with," Mountain said, as he stepped into the water. He didn't go straight in, he put his pants into the water and washed them as best he could. They were caked with mud and sweat. The bottoms were well frayed, the legs ripped in various places. The female was embarrassed by his nudity, so he would continue to wear them. It was about to be dark so she wouldn't see much of him.

Page yelped behind him.

"It's freezing but you'll feel good afterward," he said as he put the newly washed pants on the pebbled bank. He noticed she had moved back. "The fire is blazing back at camp. You will be able to get warm."

She made a little noise of agreement. "I might have to sit *in* the fire."

Mountain laughed. "It's not that bad," he said, wading in. "See." He plunged into the water, scrubbing at the main parts that needed cleaning, finishing up on his head. He rubbed a hand over his face and through his hair. By the time he came up, his skin felt numb and tingly. Mountain stood up, feeling the water cascade down him. He sucked in a breath. His feet and legs felt frozen. Everything above the waterline – from mid-thigh up – felt warm and tingly. He ran a hand through his hair and over his face, wiping away all the water as he walked from the bank.

Page stood rooted to the spot. She had that same

intense look of rapture on her face. Her eyes were glued to his cock. She was fucking beautiful in the fading late. All of her naked curves on display for—He looked away. He'd promised himself he wasn't going to stare, even if she was fucking him with her eyes.

He heard her swallow, heard her sharp intake of air.

"You'd better get in there." He used his thumb to point behind him.

"Um... I... um... I'm not sure." Then she mumbled something that sounded like *'fuck it'* and jumped in. He heard the splash, followed by a loud yell and then flailing.

Mountain held back a laugh. He didn't think she'd appreciate it if he let loose. Her eyes were wide and she was making very weird noises. Something between yelping and yelling and hissing, with a ton of teeth chattering thrown in there. She tried to run out of the water but fell, face-first, her yells drowned out as she... half-drowned!

Mountain was at her side in a second. He pulled her out of the water. Picked her up into his arms.

"Oh... oh god... oh!" Her lips were blue, her teeth chattered.

"Maybe it's too cold for humans."

"Help," she squeaked. "Cold," she managed to push out, her teeth clattering noisily.

He held her firmly against him. Trying hard to ignore how good she felt. It would be wrong to notice how hard her nipples were. How fucking amazing she felt plastered against him. Wet on wet. Page might be against the naked transferal of heat – especially when it involved his body – but right then, she wasn't complaining.

Mountain pushed all those thoughts aside and headed for the fire. He sat as close as he could get them to the flames, throwing on a few logs. All the while, he cradled her in his arms. She held on tightly. Her arms around him, her eyes squeezed closed. Her teeth still clattering all the while.

It took a few long minutes for her mouth to turn pink, for the clattering to slow down. "I guess it may have been a bit cold," he said.

"You t-think?" she laughed between shivers. "I guess… sh-shifters are made f-from sterner stuff." She sniffed. "I thought I was going to d-die there for a s-second." Her teeth still gave a chatter here or there. "If you hadn't f-fished me out, I might have d-drowned. My legs stopped w-working. They were n-numb."

"It's run-off from the mountains… in other words, it was ice not so long ago."

"N-no wonder!"

"Hey, guess what?" He smiled at her. "You smell like smoke again. Turns out you nearly died from hypothermia and all for nothing."

Page laughed. The sound made him feel warm inside. "Th-thanks for nothing." She smacked him on the side of the arm. And then a second time.

He laughed as well, holding onto her with one arm while trying to fend off her blows with the other.

The realization happened all at once, and to both of them. How close they were. How soft she felt. How hard he was. How intimate this was.

Page sucked in a breath. He heard her heartrate pick up speed. He felt her body tense. He swore to god he felt her nipples tighten against his chest, even though they were already hard.

His nostrils flared as he scented her arousal. If she'd

been a dragon female, she would have scented his too. Smelled the testosterone as it hit his bloodstream. Mountain didn't think, he just acted. In that moment, there were no slayers, no sides, no stupid-ass break-ups or asshole ex-boyfriends. There was nothing but her lips, which he captured with his mouth. Her beautiful, succulent lips.

Page moaned as he deepened the kiss. She pressed herself more firmly against him, if that was even possible, and moaned a second time. This one deeper than the first. He clutched the back of her head, feeling her wet hair in his fingers.

He made a groaning noise, one born of need. A deep-seated urgent craving, not just to rut – although he wanted that too – but for so much more. He wanted to know this female... everything about her. Mountain wanted to help her. He didn't know if Alex Bell would turn out to be something other than the evil slayer he knew her to be. Page hadn't spoken to the female in a whole decade. A lot could change in that time. He wanted to be there to pick up the pieces if things turned out badly.

He cupped her lush ass, pulling her closer, she rocked against him, making a mewling noise that drove him nuts. The friction of her body against his dick made him grunt. "I want to make you come," he whispered. "Really badly."

Page made a sound of agreement, her eyes were hazy with lust. Mountain nuzzled her neck, nipping at her flesh. He scanned the immediate area, noticing a grassy patch a little way from the fire. He planned on keeping her warm with his mouth and his hands. When he was done with her, she'd be dripping with sweat and as hot as hell.

He picked her up and within a stride or two was laying

her down. Mountain dipped his head down, taking one of her nipples into his mouth. He squeezed her other breast and by claw, but she felt so damned good. He was beyond tempted to get her all riled up and then to fuck her. To put her on her knees and give her the orgasm of her life. His balls pulled painfully tight just thinking about sinking into her warmth. Just thinking about feeling her channel clutching him like a velvety glove. In the end, Mountain ignored his own needs.

He slid down her gorgeous as fuck body and zoned in on her already swollen clit. Page choked out a cry as he suckled her. He could scent her arousal. It drove him wild. He focused all of that energy on her. He laved at her clit a good couple of times before easing his tongue into her pussy. She moaned, sounding shocked.

Fuck but she tasted amazing. He fucked her with his tongue, moving back to her clit which he sucked before softly circling the nub with his tongue. Just like before, she clutched at his hair, first with one hand and then with both. Her moans and groans turning deep and guttural and then high-pitched and keening. Thank scale he'd gone a little further off the beaten track than initially planned. He loved hearing her moans and cries. He was tempted to bring her to completion quickly like she seemed to want, but he resisted the urge. Her orgasm would be that much stronger if he made her wait for it. Mountain glanced up as he licked around the edge of her clit, her head was thrown back. Her eyes wide, her mouth open. She gasped for air. "Oh god! Please," she groaned.

Mountain bit back a smile as she tugged his hair, trying to pull him closer. She hooked a leg over his shoulder. He sucked on her for a second or two before laving around her nub again. Then he licked her slit... slowly... very slowly. All the way down to her channel and then back again, skirting around her clit like before.

She groaned deeply, sounding frustrated. It wasn't long and she was hooking a second leg over his shoulder. Her knees were somewhere in the vicinity of his ears. Every so often he licked over her clit and she would buck against his mouth and give a yell.

Mountain kept her on edge for a while, licking her nub or thrusting his tongue into her pussy here and there. Wet dripped down from her channel. He might be bald after this but it would be worth it. All worth it. When her moans turned to desperate yelps and groans, he pulled back. "I didn't finish checking for that tracker."

Despite his balls feeling like they were about to burst, he smiled against her when she moaned, "Huh?" She even glanced up, her eyes glassy, like she was drunk. Her lips swollen and pink from chewing on them or maybe from their scorching kiss. Probably from both.

"Tracker?" She frowned, both confusion and need warring with her features.

"Oh, yes." He slid a finger inside her tight pussy a couple of times.

Page moaned deeply, her back coming off the ground, her hand pulling at his hair, her hips thrusting. "Oh yes... yes... cheeccck... muuuust..." she groaned each word.

Then moaned in frustration when he removed the finger, which was nicely coated in her juices. Then he closed his mouth over her clit, keeping the suction soft. He eased the finger into her ass.

"Oh no! God... no..." He suckled her more firmly, throwing in some tongue action as well. Mountain thrust in and out of her rear hole. Not too deep, not too hard, there… just like that. Page tensed up her legs, her hand clenched his hair enough to make his eyes water. Her legs gripped him, her heels digging into his back. He kept sucking and licking, kept pumping in and out of her tight little hole. He pushed another finger into her pussy. Knowing without a doubt that it would guarantee her going off like a rocket.

Then she screamed, her back came off the ground a second time. Her scream grew louder and deeper, her fingers dug into his scalp, her heels dug deeper into his back, her pelvis thrust against him… she all out fucked his face. She stayed there for a bit, the scream turning into a long-drawn out keen. He kept at her for a while, making sure she rode it out. As she began to come down, he first eased out one finger and then the other, keeping his mouth on her until she fell back, slumped and satisfied. Her heavy breathing filled the whole clearing.

Mountain licked his lips, tasting her there. His balls ached, he was going to have to take care of this raging need. He was used to making his hand work for him, so it was nothing new.

Page lay there for a few long minutes. Her eyes closed, her breathing slowly normalizing.

"Are you okay?" He frowned, leaning over her so that he could brush the hair from her face. Her eyelids fluttered.

"You were right," Page giggled, she sounded on the verge of being drunk. Slurring a little.

Good! It meant he'd done his job right. "About what?"

"About Shaun being a jerk." She lifted herself onto her elbows. "About why he wants to take this break. He is a selfish asshole. Do you know that the only time I ever," she bit on her lower lip, "I ever... you know... orgasmed," she finally blurted, "was when I..." Her cheeks heated, and she took a deep breath. "Was when I helped myself along."

Mountain felt every muscle rope and tighten. It didn't come as a surprise.

"Do you know he used lube? Lube! Can you believe that? He told me I had a problem. That it was my fault he had to use the stuff."

"I have no idea what lube is." Mountain shook his head.

"Of course you don't." She sounded angry. Then she gave him a quick, sad smile. "I mean that in a good way. He didn't even take the time to get me ready before sex. He told me it was me who had the problem. If I didn't get wet within five seconds of us kissing, he'd pull on a condom and grab the lube and then—"

"Condom?" Mountain struggled to understand. "I thought you were engaged. You were sure as hell in a long relationship. Why did you need condoms?"

"I'm on birth control. I don't know why. I guess he's always been worried about getting me pregnant."

"But if you are in a loving relationship." He raised his brows. "It shouldn't matter if you become with child."

"That's just it!" She shook her head. "I'm beginning to realize that maybe things weren't so great between us. Sure, he was there when I needed him. He helped me get a job, get my life on track. Things were good in the beginning. Then again, maybe I was desperate for companionship. I know I was tired of being on my own. Maybe he isn't the wonderful guy I always thought he was."

"It's not like you had the best role model."

She shook her head. "Definitely not. Now... after this..." Page licked her lips. "I always just figured that I wasn't that into sex. That it wasn't 'all that,' but I was wrong. I thought there might be something wrong with me, but it turns out," her gaze landed on his cock, "I'm just fine. I *can* get turned on. I *can* have orgasms. Amazing orgasms. Maybe it isn't just the sex that was a problem. There's nothing wrong with wearing sexy underwear and sexy clothes. There's nothing wrong with having that second glass of wine and getting a little bit tipsy at a party or talking too loud..." She looked him in the eyes. "Shaun cares a great deal about what other people think of him. He might have been... make that, he *is* too controlling. I think Jenna was right."

"Who's Jenna?" he asked.

"My friend. My very dear and wonderful friend. Maybe Jenna was right all along about Shaun."

"You keep saying maybe."

"It's just hard to think straight right now, out here... with you. After that... wow!!! I mean..." She pushed out a laden breath.

Mountain didn't know what to say to that. Page had to make those decisions for herself much as he wanted to tell her that she was right on the money. He didn't need to meet this Shaun asshole to know it was true. Ultimately, she needed to figure this out for herself. She needed to trust her gut.

Her eyes moved back to his cock, which was still painfully hard. It jutted from between his legs, his balls were still sitting pretty much in his throat as well. She licked her lips as she moved onto all fours, crawling over to him, a feral look in her eyes.

"Maybe this isn't—"

She gave him a shove and he allowed himself to fall back. Then, she straddled him, her eyes still on his member... they were filled with hunger. "Maybe this isn't a good idea," he forced himself to say through gritted teeth.

Page was a beautiful female. Her hair was wild. It tumbled down her back. Her eyes were stunning, especially when filled with such desire – and for him, all for him. But were they? Or was this something else. Did this have something to do with her ex?

She pulled her shoulders back, her full tits commanded his attention. All thought of *what's his name* fled. Her pink nipples begged to be sucked. Her hips were beautifully flared, her thighs so damned lush. She leaned in... preparing to suck him off.

Suck.

Him.

He groaned, long before she ever made contact. It was a sound of frustration. He couldn't allow this. Couldn't let her do it, she wasn't in the right frame of mind. "You shouldn't... we should talk about this..."

She kept on coming. Her lips parted, her breathing picked up, her eyes stayed glued to his cock.

He tried again. "Let's disc—" he hissed when she gripped him by the base of his cock. Then groaned when she closed her mouth over him. Then he was threading his fingers through her hair and pulling her in closer. His eyes rolling back into his scalp. "You shouldn't!" He made one last ditch effort. She deep-throated him. "Page... shit... um..." He watched her mouth work him. Up and down on his cock, while her hand jerked him off using firm, even strokes.

He had been trying to prolong her pleasure. Page had no such qualms. His cock hit the back of her throat and he grunted. "You don't have to…" he ground out, his voice deep and gravelly.

Her response was to take him deeper, quicker. He had to work to keep from fisting her hair, from fucking her sweet mouth. "Feels… good… oh… fuck!" Sweat accumulated on his brow.

She moved up and down rhythmically, her tits rocked back and forth in time with the motion. Mountain was so damned tempted to pick her up and to put her on his cock. To wring another orgasm from her. He held back. His brain was foggy but he somehow managed to compute that it wouldn't be a good idea.

His balls were pulling tighter, that coiling sensation was building in his body.

"Mountain!" a male yelled. "What the fuck!" he added with a snarl.

Mountain jumped to his feet, putting himself between his female and the unknown male. The foe. The enemy. It took him three long seconds to realize who it was. "Smoke? What the fuck are you doing here?" He took a step forward, making sure the male's attention was on him.

"What am *I* doing here?" Smoke shook his head. "I should be asking you that question, along with, 'who is the female?'" Smoke tried to look past Mountain, but he stayed where he was.

Mountain glanced back at Page. She stayed facing the opposite direction, hugging herself to try to cover her naked body. Hopefully Smoke hadn't gotten a good look.

"She's mine," Mountain snarled, shocked at the possession he heard in his voice.

Smoke frowned. "That can't be—"

Mountain could see that he was thinking hard. "All of the hunt females were accounted for. Every…" His eyes widened. "Who is that?" he demanded, using a harsh tone this time. "She had better not be who I think she is." His voice turned deep and accusing. "It can't be though." He frowned.

Page whimpered.

Mountain growled, widening his stance and preparing to do battle. *Little snot!* The male needed to be put in his place. He might be one of the higher-ranking Fire dragons, but he was no match for Mountain. He worked hard to compose himself. He didn't want Page getting hurt. "Let's go over there and talk," he suggested, nodding to the other side of the clearing.

Smoke narrowed his eyes. "There isn't much to discuss. You shouldn't be here with a human."

"Let's go over there," Mountain growled. "It would be the best thing to do right now."

Smoke held his gaze for a few more moments before conceding.

Mountain glanced back at Page, she was still facing the other way with her body. She had her head turned towards him. He noticed that the fire had burned down and how dark it was getting. He added a few logs to the fire. "I'll be back in a minute."

She nodded, her eyes fearful.

"It'll be okay," he tried to reassure her.

She nodded again.

"I told you I'd protect you and I will," he added.

Thank claw, some of the fear left her eyes.

"What's going on?" Smoke growled from the other side of the clearing as he approached. "I hope you have a good explanation.

Fucking fire-breathers. They pissed him the hell off. Mountain outranked this male. If the little fucker thought a few flames were going to scare him, idiot could think again. Mountain pulled in a deep breath, trying to calm the fuck down. He needed to first try to talk his way out of this. It would be safer for Page. Even though they were a little distance away, he didn't want her getting hurt. If that didn't work though... Well, he'd do what he needed to do. Smoke had better have brought his A-game.

CHAPTER 10

*O*h *shit!*
　　Holy freaking crap balls!
This was not good. Not good at all. The guy who had come crashing in on them looked pissed. He looked to be in his mid-twenties with dark hair and bright blue eyes. His face was either clean-shaven or soft like a baby's bum. She wasn't sure which, only that he had nothing on Mountain who was way bigger, way stronger and well… she could see he could kick the younger guy's ass in half a second flat.

Mine.

The word kept rolling around in her head. More like charging. Yep, charging was a better word. Even better yet, stampeding. Why had he called her his? Especially when that wasn't true. She was barely out of a relationship with Shaun. There must be some logical explanation. *Yes!* Now that she thought about it, she was sure there was a very good reason he had proclaimed ownership of her. Maybe like a prisoner or something.

She huddled up, curled around herself, hugging her arms around her body, hoping that the shifter hadn't gotten too much of an eyeful. Her cheeks heated and she felt like groaning with sheer embarrassment. Page was sure he had seen everything. That he'd seen her giving Mountain a blowjob. That he'd seen her naked. Her ass in the air. Her mouth… She turned to the other side of the clearing and watched as Mountain strode away from her. He'd said it would be okay. He'd promised to protect her, and she believed him.

The other shifter said something, his face animated, he glared in her direction. Mountain said something back, just as animated.

The shifter, Smoke, didn't like it because he shook his head. They argued for a minute or so. It seemed like forever. Back and forth, becoming more and more heated.

Smoke said something that looked very much like "Fuck that!" Then he said something else that had Mountain shaking his head.

"Move!" Smoke yelled, loud enough for her to hear.

Mountain said something back that the shifter didn't like, judging by the scowl that contorted his face. Smoke tried to shove Mountain aside. The guy's eyes were on her. Page realized with horror that he was trying to get to her. Thank god Mountain was having none of that.

"Move or—" Smoke snarled.

Mountain punched the shifter square in the face. There was a loud crunch and blood sprayed. Page gasped. The shifter staggered back. He put his arms out to try to rebalance.

A plume of fire erupted from his throat. Luckily, he was facing the canopy or Mountain's face would have melted right then. Instead, Mountain punched the guy again, this time in the throat. There was another sickening crunch and the guy went down.

She was sure Mountain was done, because Smoke looked done. The fight looked over to her, but obviously Mountain didn't agree because he kicked Smoke in the ribs.

She flinched at the dull thud, flinching again when he kicked him a second time. This time there was a crack along with the thud.

"Stop!" she yelled.

His back tensed and he turned to her. His expression was one of rage. It instantly softened as he took her in. His chest heaved. It was a terrible thought to have in that moment, but he looked beautiful. Utterly terrifying. Devastatingly gorgeous. Rage and aggression should not be sexy, but it was on Mountain. He pulled it off and then some.

"I had to put him down," Mountain said as strode towards her. "Had to be sure he stays down – at least for a couple of hours. We need to leave."

"Are you going to shift now?"

"I told you I can't." He shook his head, walking over to where she sat.

"Do you still need time to get to know me?" She frowned. "Is that it? Don't you trust me yet?"

"I trust you, Page. The problem is that the rest of my people won't."

"I still don't understand."

He held his hand out and she took it. Mountain hoisted her to her feet.

"You can shift and can have us back in no time. Am I

missing something? Why did you say I was yours just now?"

"I told you that you need to trust me. The only way I can protect you is if I make it back on my own steam. I can't shift. That's all I'm going to tell you right now." He pushed out a breath.

"On your own steam?" she frowned again.

"Like this," he looked down at himself, "in my human form. We need to move. The time for a leisurely hike back is gone. I need to take the most direct route. I need to get us back before it's too late."

"Too late for what?" She was baffled by what he was saying. She didn't like it one bit. Why didn't he want to tell her what he had planned?

"When we get there, you can't argue. You need to go with it. Do everything I say. Agree to everything."

"Tell me what everything is. I can't just agree to—"

"We don't have time to discuss this." He let frustration bleed into his words. "We don't have time to argue right now. If you want me to help you, you don't have a choice."

"I'm not going to like this plan of yours, am I?"

He got this pained look.

Page scrubbed a hand over her face. "I'm going to hate it. I can tell. That's why you won't talk to me about it."

"If Smoke makes it back before us, we're in deep fucking shit. More dragons will come. Too many! They will take you, and I won't be able to protect you any longer. We don't have time for me to spell this out for you. I was hoping we would, but we don't."

"I don't like it." She shook her head.

"Trust me, okay? You asked me to trust you and now I'm asking the same from you." He cupped her cheek, his chestnut eyes boring into hers.

She finally nodded. "Okay. Yes, I trust you. God help me, but I do."

"Thank you." He kissed her. It was quick. A brush of the lips. Then he was picking her up. "We'll get our clothing. When we get back to the lair though, you need to know, we're finishing this." His deep voice sent shivers down her spine.

Her mouth instantly felt dry. Her throat clogged. She nodded once but he was already running. Moving faster than she thought possible.

When they reached the river, he put her down and she dressed quickly, her fingers fumbling.

Mountain tried to hand her back her glasses. She shook her head. "I don't need them."

He frowned.

"I can see just fine. The glasses were a disguise, remember? Actually, I think I might see better without them."

Mountain gave her a half-smile as he picked her up, hoisting her onto his back. Then he was running like his ass was on fire.

CHAPTER 11

It felt really early. Or really late. Page wasn't sure which. All she knew was that she was exhausted. Totally finished. She kept trying to nod off, which was impossible perched on Mountain's back. She had to hold on or she was going to fall.

They'd been on the move for hours. Stopping for a handful of minutes here and there so that they could relieve themselves or drink from a stream. It felt like forever since they'd last stopped. Her legs hurt. Her hands hurt. Everything felt stiff and sore. Her eyes hurt the most. They felt dry and scratchy.

Page felt bad for complaining – even though she only did it inside her own head. How must poor Mountain be feeling? He was the one carrying her. He was the one having to run. She was shocked at how fast he was. How agile and quiet. Covering miles and miles of ground silently and quickly.

Then he stopped. It happened so suddenly she almost let go of him.

"We're here," he announced, looking up.

She tracked his line of vision. They were at the base of a tall cliff. There were—*No! Wait a minute... Yes!* There were lights blinking up there. In the actual cliff. "Is that it?" she asked, sounding in awe, which was appropriate because it was how she felt. Totally in awe of what she was seeing. Balconies and windows built into the side of a mountain.

"My lair." He slowly lowered her onto shaky legs.

"I need to get you up there. Remember what I said, Page." He sounded stern, looked stern. "You do not let go of my hand and you must not argue. You need to agree with everything I say. We can argue about it once we are in my chamber. If you go against me, they will take you. I will have no say." He shook his head. "I won't be able to help you. As it stands, we have a fight on our hands."

"Fine! I'm sure it can't be that hectic."

His jaw tensed and his eyes got a look she didn't like. Then he was moving away from her. There was a shift in the actual air. A static, followed by cracking noises. She watched as his limbs stretched.

Holy shit!

His jaw elongated. Scales sprouted, along with a tail. A long, forked tail. The process was quick. A few seconds later and a magnificent beast stood before her. He was bigger than the one who had blown her helicopter out of the sky. Then again, this was Mountain. His eyes were the only things she recognized. The same color only brighter, more vivid. That, and his pupils were slitted instead of round. *Beautiful.*

He growled, flapping his great wings. His huge, muscular body lifted. Then he was grabbing her in his talons and flying up. She yelped, feeling both fearful and exhilarated.

She heard shouts and growls, from above her. Men – make that shifters – were pointing at them. A whole lot of them were assembled on a huge balcony. They parted, giving Mountain space to land. She saw two of them had golden chests. Page could still remember what that meant. They were royalty.

A hush fell over the crowd as they landed. Touching down right in front of the two royal guys. She wondered if one of them was the king.

"It's her!" someone shouted.

"It's that slayer," someone else growled, sounding angry. They spoke in hushed tones.

She watched as one of the royal dragons sniffed the air. He frowned. "What the fuck!" he bellowed, looking shocked. "I was sure the Fire dragon was talking shit!" he added.

Forget taking her hand, Mountain hooked an arm around her waist and pulled her in close, so that her back was flush against his front. When had he shifted back into his human form? She had been too busy watching the others, especially the royal dragons, to pay much attention.

"What is going on?" the one with the dark hair said. He had even darker eyes, which narrowed on her as he spoke to Mountain.

"You're fucking with a slayer?" the other one barked. "This has to be a joke." He sniffed the air again.

"This is my female," Mountain growled out the words. "I would urge you to have some respect, my lord." Although Mountain spoke calmly, his body felt tense against her.

My female. My. Female. Back to that whole *'mine'* thing again.

What the heck was going on?

The lighter-haired one snorted out a mirthless laugh. "Tell me another one." He tried to hand Mountain a pair of pants. They were neatly folded. Mountain ignored him.

"Your female?" the darker-haired one frowned. "I don't think so. You had better explain and you had better make it quick."

"Happily, my king."

Oh! So, the dark one was the king. Interesting. She felt like maybe she should curtsey or bow or something. She settled with staying still and keeping quiet, like Mountain had asked her. Besides, she couldn't move much in his strong grasp.

"I hunted this female, I captured her, marked her and plan on claiming her as soon as I get to my chamber. She is mine!" He snarled the last, his arm tightening around her a fraction.

Mine.

There he went again. *Claiming?* What did that even mean? Page kept quiet. She trusted Mountain. If this was what it took to save her ass, then so be it.

"It's what I was trying to do when Smoke interrupted us."

The fairer royal smirked. "It sounded to me like you were trying to *claim* her mouth."

Oh god! He hadn't just said that.

A couple of the guys snickered, a few more laughed. Some of them talked.

Mountain growled low, she felt his chest vibrate against her back. "You will not mock my female, Shale, or so fucking help me I'll—"

The light-haired guy held up his hand. "I apologize." Then he frowned. "This female is on our wanted list. She is a slayer. What are you doing? Have you lost your mind? I know it's been a while since the last Stag Run, but... a slayer? Her?" His eyes flicked to Page and then back to Mountain. "I'll give it to you that she's sexy."

Mountain growled low, sounding like a wild animal.

The cocky royal ignored Mountain. "Fucking around with a slayer though, even a sexy one, is sick," he added.

"This particular female wasn't even part of the hunt," the king said. "I'm happy you captured her, but I'm afraid I can't let you claim her. I'm going to have to contact Blaze. I want her imprisoned until he gets here to question her."

"No!" Mountain snarled. "This isn't Alex Bell. She isn't on the list."

"Don't talk shit." Shale interrupted him. "I'm sorry but you can't keep her. I'm sure she gives great head—"

Whop!

Mountain's fist shot out. It connected with Shale's chin and the guy staggered back, his face a mask of shock. "What the—?" he managed, rubbing his jaw. "You can't hit me!" he snarled. "I'm your superior."

"I warned you not to mock my female again and I meant it. You don't know what the fuck you are talking about. This is Page Bell, Alex's sister. She isn't a slayer. She left the organization ten years ago. She has a normal life and I can prove it. I hunted her, captured her and now she is mine. I wish to claim her and then mate her."

She sucked in a breath. "Um—"

He squeezed her hip and she shut her mouth. *What the*

hell! Mate? Had he said 'mate'?

"I was in the process of claiming her when Smoke interrupted – don't you dare open your mouth," he directed the last at Shale who raised his brows.

"I hadn't planned on it." He moved his jaw from side to side. "I like my bones intact. You broke three of my ribs at the start of the hunt."

"Good! You—" Mountain began.

"Okay," the king interrupted. "Let's just say this *is* Page – Alex's sister..." the king scrutinized her, not looking like he believed a word. "Let's say she isn't a slayer. You still have no place claiming or mating her. She isn't up for grabs."

Up for grabs?

Mating?

What the hell was going on?

Mountain squeezed her hip again. Had she tensed up? Made a strange noise? It was quite possible. Then she realized that Mountain didn't actually mean any of it. He didn't see her as his. He didn't plan on mating her. That was laughable. Totally absurd. In fact, she had to bite back a giggle at the thought of something so utterly crazy. They had barely known each other for three days. Three measly days. He was just saying all of it to get her out of shit street. She could relax and breathe more easily.

"Blaze said that the humans were out there. He said we should hunt and capture them. He never specified who exactly they were. He didn't name names. He just said human females. Then he laid down the rules which I followed to the letter. Here is my human – captured and marked – soon to be claimed. I won her fair and square. When Smoke tried to take her, I put him down. Let any of you try to take her from me and I will take you down as well."

The king widened his eyes. "Blaze wasn't talking about any random female. He was talking about the ones who had signed up, the ones who—"

"He never specified!" Mountain's chest vibrated. His voice was deep and resonating. "All he said was human. That was it."

"Okay. I will have to take it up with him. As to the female—" The king looked at her.

"*My* female!" Mountain sounded a bit like a caveman. She could feel how tense his muscles were.

"About… *your* female," the king said, looking unsure, "how positive are you that she isn't Alex Bell? I'm not sure I trust your judgment right now. I don't think you're thinking clearly."

"I studied that photograph of Alex Bell – we all did." He cleared his throat. "I noticed subtle differences. My female does not have the hand marking. The mark of the slayers. She left the organization before one could be placed onto her." Mountain gripped her wrist and held up the hand in question. "See. You can look at both of them." She held up the other one for him to see. Shale studied her hands, but the king kept his eyes on Mountain.

"Look at that," Shale remarked. "She doesn't have the mark. What does that mean? She looks just like Alex."

"They are identical twins… twins, okay? Surely we of all dragons can understand that?"

"She could have removed the marking. I have heard of humans doing that," the king spat.

"Her hair is too long to be Alex Bell," Mountain tried. "There are other differences."

Her boobs. She cringed. *'Please don't mention them here in front of everyone,'* she silently begged. Shale looked her up and down... up and down, slowly... slowly.

"She looks just like Alex Bell to me. I'm not convinced." The king shook his head. "I think she has you wrapped around her finger. I don't think anything you have shown us is conclusive."

Up and down... up and—Shale's eyes widened. They were glued to her chest. "Oh shit! This isn't Alex. I believe you, bro. I'm sorry I doubted." He laughed. "Twins! How bizarre. They are identical, just like—"

"How can you possibly tell?" the king interrupted. "You're just saying that because Mountain is your friend."

Shale and Mountain were friends? They didn't act like friends.

"Friendship has nothing to do with it. Alex has a better rack." Shale put his hands up over his chest, pretending to grope imaginary breasts. "Not by much, I must add but—"

"Bull-fucking-shit!" Mountain growled. "My female has amazing breasts."

Alex felt her cheeks heat, she wanted to die right there on the spot.

"What are you talking about?" the king asked.

Shale chuckled. "This definitely isn't Alex Bell," he spoke to the king. "Aside from the hand marking and the hair, her..." He gestured to her boobs with his head and eyes.

Page folded her arms across her chest, wishing the ground would open and swallow her.

"Don't!" Mountain warned.

"Certain areas are not as well en—"

"I said not to fucking go there," Mountain rasped.

"Okay, okay." The king held up both hands. "You're sure?" he asked Shale.

"A bit touchy, Mountain?" Shale chuckled.

"Fuck you!" Mountain snarled.

"I'm very sure." Shale was grinning broadly. "I'm just teasing you, bro."

"It doesn't mean she's not a slayer," the king said. Ignoring Shale's jabs.

Page had to stop herself from rolling her eyes.

"She's not!" Mountain growled. "I will prove it soon enough!"

"Even if she isn't a slayer, it doesn't mean you can keep her."

She felt Mountain tense. She heard him pull in a breath.

"Don't say it! This isn't going to be my decision. I will contact Blaze and discuss it with him. Blaze is in charge of the hunt. Whatever he decides will be final."

She could hear Mountain grind his teeth.

"What will happen to me?" Page asked.

The king turned those hard, dark eyes on her. In that moment she was thankful that Mountain was there. "You will need to prove that you are not a slayer. We will then release you back into human territory."

No more Mountain.

No more… this… whatever they had going. Probably nothing but she felt a pang at the thought anyway. She finally nodded.

"Why are you here? Why did you come?" The king narrowed his eyes. He still didn't believe her.

"I came to find my sister. To find Alex. I was told that she helped a dragon escape. That they were possibly partners, that they might have a relationship. I assumed they would have come into dragon territory. That they would be hiding here. I decided to take a chopper into your territory. I was unarmed. I realized that I might be unsuccessful. In fact, it was probably a stupid thing to do. I never ever thought I'd be shot from the sky."

The king pushed out a breath. "That does tie in with some information that came through a few days ago. Beck has left his people to be with a slayer... Alex, your sister. She and Beck are in a relationship."

"What?" Mountain gasped "He left?"

The king nodded. "Your female here was blown from the sky and Beck thought it was Alex. By all accounts he was stricken. Took off like his ass was on fire. Initially, we all thought she died in the crash. After hearing from him, we assumed a random female had been killed. It turned out to be you... and you didn't die. It's all quite confusing."

"I almost did," Page mumbled. "Who is Beck?" she asked, knowing the answer.

"One of the Water dragons," Shale answered. "The dragon Alex captured. The one she helped escape."

"See!" Page said. "I told you she left the organization." She turned to Mountain. "I told you she helped him. She's a good person. They *are* together."

Mountain was frowning heavily, he looked to be deep in thought. His eyes brightened as they landed on her. He looked back at the king. "Beck would not leave to be in a relationship with a female who is evil. He wouldn't want to be with a slayer. Beck is a hard male. He would eat someone like that for breakfast. Male or female, it wouldn't matter."

"I agree," Shale said. "It doesn't compute. I couldn't see Beck being with a female who was an evil bitch." He frowned. "But maybe he has been led astray. Pussy could have that effect on a male."

The king elbowed him. Shale grunted. "It's true," he said, rubbing his arm.

"I am going to put the female in your care for now," the king said. "Just until I hear back from Blaze."

Mountain put his other arm around her. "I will fight any who try to take her." His voice was so gravelly it caused gooseflesh to rise on her arms. A shiver to run down her spine. He sounded so convincing, she almost believed the whole thing.

The king shook his head. "Do you know what you're doing, Mountain?"

"Yes." No hesitation.

"Are you sure you are thinking clearly? You have… feelings for this female?"

"Yes." Again, no hesitation. "I have feelings for her. I want to mate her."

Her heart sped up and for a moment she felt panicky. Just until she remembered that this was an act. That it wasn't real. It sounded real. In this moment it felt real, but it wasn't.

"So you keep saying," the king muttered. "I take it you checked her for a tracker? Please tell me you checked her."

"Thoroughly." Was it just her imagination or had Mountain smiled when he said that? It sounded like he had smiled. As it stood, she had to bite her lip to hold back a giggle at the thought of how Mountain had *checked* her. She had to bite harder when she thought about how *thoroughly* he had gone about it.

The king frowned. "Good. Guard her. She is your responsibility. You may not claim her though."

Mountain growled, sounding like a lion, or a cougar or something. "I *have* been guarding her and will continue to do so. I don't want to wait with the claiming. I wish to claim her as soon as we get to my chamber. It will be safer that way."

"It is no use claiming her if you can't have her. I am sure we will hear from Blaze soon." Pity clouded his face. "No one will try to take her – not until we know for sure."

"You don't expect for the news to be good," Mountain said.

"Depends on what you would call good."

"You know what I mean." Mountain sounded irritated. "This is my female. You don't think I'm going to be permitted to keep her. Being told I have to give her up would be… a problem for me." His jaw worked.

"No," the king shook his head, "I would be very surprised if Blaze lets you keep her. You should prepare for the worst." He shrugged once, that look of pity back.

"I want to talk to him," Mountain growled, sounding more like an animal. "I wish to plead my case."

"Allow me," Shale said. "I will talk to Blaze on your behalf. You are too emotional about this. It might not come across in a way you would wish."

She felt Mountain relax, he even sighed. "Okay, thank you."

"No problem!" He leaned forward and tapped Mountain on the arm. "You have always been good at reading people, especially humans. I trust your judgment with this female. I will come and see you as soon as we hear from Blaze." Shale tried to hand the pants to

Mountain again. This time he took them. Shale glanced at the king. "Isn't that right, Granite?"

The king nodded. "Sit tight until then." He gave Mountain a solemn stare.

"Where is Obsidian?" It felt like Mountain had pulled back from her, like he was looking around them. That name was familiar, but she couldn't place it right then.

"Your guess is as good as ours." Shale shrugged. "You know how it is with him, the male disappears for days on end. There was a reported sighting of him near the southern quadrant. Our males have been instructed to stay away. It's safer for them that way. He can be rather testy in his scales."

"Nah, Obsidian is far testier in human form." Mountain said.

"Don't look so worried," Shale went on. "You know him. He'll turn up soon enough. Rock has been in charge during your absence. He's been running the various teams, ensuring that all our bases are covered. Keeping eyes on all corners of our territory. Not an easy task."

"Not considering how vast our territories are and how limited our resources are," Mountain spoke more to himself. "Rock will have his hands full." Mountain looked deep in thought.

"I've been helping him," Shale added. "We did end up investing in radar equipment. Blaze agreed yesterday." He smiled broadly.

Mountain smiled as well. "That's great news." Then he seemed to realize where he was. "We'll discuss it later."

Shale nodded.

Running teams? Ensuring that bases were covered? Radar equipment? "I thought you were a trainer?" she blurted the

question without thinking. "That doesn't sound very...
trainerish?"

"Training?" Shale frowned.

"Training is a major part of my role. It is the most
important part," Mountain countered.

Shale snickered. "Mountain told you he's a trainer?"

She nodded.

"You are *not* a trainer. You're trying to win this female,
buddy." Shale widened his eyes. "This is one of those
times when small dick syndrome can come in handy. You
can boast a little, you know?"

Small dick syndrome? Huh! That didn't make any sense. Page
frowned. Mountain had no problem in that department.
She wasn't sure what Shale was talking about. Loads of the
guys around them right then were naked – not that she
was looking. In fact, she was trying hard not to see them.
It couldn't be helped though. At this point, she could state
that although dragon shifters as a whole were ridiculously
well hung, Mountain still lived up to his name when it
came to his package. He lived up to it big time.

"For the last fucking time," Mountain growled. "I don't
have small dick syndrome. You need to stop with that shit.
You've used the same line for years. Ever since we were
teenagers."

Shale chuckled, locking eyes with him. "That's because
it's still funny." He looked at her. "Your boyfriend over
here is far too modest. He pretty much runs the show and
is the highest-ranking non-royal Earth dragon we have.
Every single male you see here reports to him. There are
a whole lot who aren't here right now, who do too. He's a
big deal. A trainer?" He laughed. "I don't think so."

Holy shit!

"Okay, Shale, that's enough," Mountain said. "We are headed for my chamber. My female is tired and hungry. I don't have anything to prove to anyone. I don't have small dick syndrome and had planned on telling my female more about my position as soon as I trusted her enough. When I first met her, I thought she was Alex Bell. I was then convinced for a time that she might be a slayer. I didn't trust her right off the bat. Didn't want her thinking I was anyone important."

That stung! He still didn't trust her enough. Why hadn't he set the record straight?

"Then Smoke came crashing in on us before I got the chance. Not that it's any of your business. Now, if you'll excuse us, my lord." He put a hand on her back and directed her towards the doors that led inside the lair.

Everyone's eyes were on them. The large balcony was stuffed to the gills with shifters, as was the hall inside. Mountain kept an arm around her shoulders. Most of the guys stepped out of the way, making a path for them. One or two were a little slow doing so and elicited a growl from Mountain. He was pushy and possessive and – lord help her – but… but… she liked it.

It felt like it took forever before they were finally through the doors that opened from the balcony to the lair. "Maybe we should have gone to look for Alex first," she whispered as they rushed through the hall. "Maybe we shouldn't have come here," she added, feeling nervous.

"We will talk when we reach my chamber."

CHAPTER 12

It felt like they walked for a long time. In reality it couldn't have been for more than five or ten minutes. The lair was beautiful. Nothing like she expected. Gleaming floors, bejeweled chandeliers, beautifully carved wooden doors. Rugs that looked like they might just be Persian… as in, the real deal. The hallways were long and wide. The ceilings impossibly tall.

He finally stopped and opened a door. Her jaw dropped. The views were magnificent despite it still being dark. The large expanse of star-littered sky was still enough to stop her in her tracks. To have her forgetting, just for a moment, about the dark that came along with them. Then he flicked a switch, which illuminated the apartment.

It was large and spacious. All open-plan. The bed was the main feature. It was huge, bigger than anything she'd ever seen. It had four posts and beautiful white linen. There was also a large oval tub which sat in front of the vast windows. To the right was a lounge and dining area, as well as a small kitchen along the one wall. It was modern, with a gas hob.

"The bathroom is through there." Mountain pointed at two doors. "The one on the right is the toilet. There's a shower on the left, unless you want to take a bath. It would be great for soothing sore muscles. I could run you a bubble bath, get the jets going."

"Sounds good." It did. It sounded heavenly. "What about you though?"

He smiled. "I'll pop in the shower and then I'll order some food while you are relaxing in the bath. A couple of steaks, unless," he raised his brows in question, "you wanted something else?"

"Steaks would be great. Thank you."

"Sure. I can see how worried you are, and I need you to know that it's going to be okay." He took her hand. "We'll work this whole thing out. I'm hopeful, even if Granite isn't confident, that Blaze will give his permission. We will be able to move freely after that. I'll be able to accompany you. I'll help you find Alex and we can get to the bottom of all this."

"Who is Blaze? He sounds important."

"He's the king of all the dragons," Mountain said.

"Oh. Granite is a king as well? There is more than one king?"

Mountain nodded. "We have four kings, one for each tribe. There's Earth," Mountain touched a hand to his chest, "I am an Earth dragon. We have dark flecks blended into our chest markings. Then there are Water dragons – Beck, your sister's mate, is a Water dragon; they have green flecks. Air dragons have blue threaded into their markings, and Fire dragons have pure golden markings. Each tribe has its own king. Blaze is a Fire dragon, he rules us all. His word is final. Fire dragons can breathe fire. We all have an ability."

"Wow! That's interesting." Page knew about their fire-breathing ability but assumed that all the dragons could do it. She couldn't remember exactly what she had been taught on the matter. "So, only Fire dragons can breathe fire?"

"Yes. At least up until recently, but that's a discussion for another day."

"Okay. I knew royal dragons had golden chests, but I had no idea beyond that. What is your ability?"

"We have the least interesting of the abilities." She waited for him to elaborate.

When he didn't, she decided to go ahead and ask. "You keep playing stuff down. Your job and now your ability. You won't even tell me what it is?"

"Fine," he sighed. "We can blend in with our surroundings. It's saved my ass a good couple of times."

"You blend in?" She frowned. "As in, like a chameleon?"

"Exactly right. Only, we are much better at it than the reptiles."

"Oh." She widened her eyes, as realization dawned. "Ohhhh! Back in the forest, when that dragon was onto us – the one who nearly found us – you covered me with your body and pressed us against a tree. Were you... camouflaging us?"

He nodded. "Yes, that's exactly what I was doing. I am able to camouflage visually and also my scent. It is why I covered you with my body."

"That's impressive." She smiled at him. "Way better than breathing fire."

He grinned. "I planned on telling you, by the way... about my job here. I needed to be careful though. I hope you understand."

Page shrugged. "You needed to make sure I wasn't hiding a tracker." She stifled a laugh, grinning instead.

"Exactly." He slid his arms around her, nuzzling her neck. "I might just need to keep checking for those. I can't... be too careful." He spoke between kisses.

His mouth felt good on her skin. He used his teeth to nip at her earlobe. It felt amazing, sending shivers through her. Mountain pulled back. "I'll go and run your bath now, before I'm tempted to... claim you." He gave her a wicked smile.

"Since you brought it up," she squeezed his hand, preventing him from pulling away completely, "thank you for saying all that. For putting yourself out there like that. I mean, you told your king – Granite – you had feelings for me." She made a face. "That you want to mate me." She laughed in a quick, nervous burst. Not because of what she was saying but because of how he was looking at her. Almost like..."I mean, it's funny, right? Because you couldn't possibly..." Why was he looking at her like she'd just trodden on his favorite toy? Stomped all over it and dumped it in the mud.

Thank god Mountain grinned just then. Thank the lord he began to chuckle along with her. For a second she'd started getting worried that maybe he had meant it.

"We don't even know one another," she giggled. "No wonder he's finding it hard to swallow."

Mountain kept on laughing. "Actually," he was grinning broadly, "it's not so hard to swallow. Shifters don't mess around when it comes to these things."

She bit back her laugh. He couldn't be serious. "Yeah, but so soon? Come on, really?"

"When I told you we don't mess around, I meant it. Seven years of courtship would never happen. I don't say that to hurt you."

She made a snorting noise. "I know that." He'd mentioned it before. Heck, seven years was long for anyone.

"Seven *weeks* would be a long time for a shifter. Seven days… now that's more our style."

"Days?" Her eyes widened. He had mentioned something along those lines before but… it couldn't be.

"All I have done is, hopefully, bought us some time. That's if I get the go-ahead. Let's wait and see what happens. We can discuss it once we hear back. You should get out of those clothes." She watched as he walked to the tub and turned the faucet on. Listened as water began to run into it with an initial splatter. "I'll get you something clean to wear," he said over his shoulder as he poured some foam bath into the tub.

Shaun wouldn't have been this caring. If anything, it would have been the other way around. Her running after him. Her waiting on him. Shaun would have sat his ass down and that would have been the end of it. Why hadn't she seen it before? There had been very little give and take in their relationship.

"Thank you." She smiled at him.

Mountain was sweet and kind and… he was great. She realized that this was the first time she had thought about Shaun in a while. For once, Page didn't feel sad or upset or angry like she normally would. She didn't feel much of anything. Was it indifference, or something else though?

He fetched her a towel and a robe, which looked like it would be miles too big for her. Then he searched through a closet, finally returning with a t-shirt. "This should be fine to sleep in."

"That's perfect."

He ordered their food while she undressed. Page stepped into the bath; the water was amazing. She held back a groan of pleasure as she sank into the suds. "Wow!" she pushed out as she sank back against the side of the tub. "That's magnificent." Her eyes were on the view. The sun had just begun to show above the horizon. Light shimmered and danced over the ocean. The sky was an array of purples. From a light lavender to an inky wine hue. Stars still shone brightly.

"Sure is," Mountain said, eyes on the view. "I never tire of seeing it." He kept looking for a few moments and then pulled down his cotton pants, stepping out of them as he headed for the bathroom. His ass was meaty, his back wide and muscular.

Page watched, slack-jawed until he disappeared behind the door, which he left ajar. She heard the water splatter to life and allowed herself to sink under the water. It was something she loved to do as a child. Lie in the bath, water to just over her ears, eyes closed. Warm and comforting. She could hear her heart beating and the swishing and swirling of the water.

Page lay like that for a good couple of minutes but began to feel sleepy. It would be better if she washed up and got out before she fell asleep. She put her hand up, feeling around for the soap. There! She clutched it, pulling her hand back into the water and opened her eyes.

Oh!

She blinked a couple of times. Mountain stood over the tub looking down at her. He was frowning heavily. He looked angry. His jaw was tensed, his eyes narrowed. His muscles had that bulging, roped look he got when he was upset. Why would he be upset? He was naked and bristling.

She slowly came up out of the water, staying under for the most part. "Are you okay?" She frowned.

He grunted something that sounded like 'yes' and then sniffed at her. As in, he leaned forward, hovering over her head and arms, which were the only parts of her out of the water and sniffed loudly. He made another grunting noise.

"What's wrong?" she asked, since he was beginning to scare her. "You okay?" she added again.

She noticed that despite having gone to shower, his hair was still dry. *Why was his hair dry?* Also, she could still hear the sound of the water running in the bathroom. *Had he decided not to get in? Why not?*

She allowed her gaze to track down his body. Down... down... *Oh shit!* This wasn't—

"Obsidian," Mountain growled from the door. He sounded both shocked and pissed.

Thank goodness she was in a bathtub with plenty of bubbles or... Page covered herself under the soap suds as the guy who looked exactly like Mountain continued to stare down at her, eyes narrowed, muscles bulging. *Holy crap!* He looked like he could do some real damage.

"What the hell are you doing here? Why the fuck didn't you knock first?" Mountain asked. It sounded like he was closer. "We talked about this."

Obsidian shrugged, looking, if anything, angrier.

"Don't tell me..." Mountain shook his head, walking

further into the room. His hair was wet, and he wore a towel. It hung low around his hips. "You didn't come through the door, did you? You came in via the balcony?"

Obsidian shrugged. "Yes," he ground out, his voice deep and gravelly. Barely human. Mountain had said that his brother was more animal than man. A shiver ran down her spine and not in a good way this time.

"You are scaring my female," Mountain said. "From now on you will have to use the front door." He pointed in the general direction. "You'll have to knock."

Mountain's brother growled, looking like he didn't particularly like the idea. She noted a flash of his teeth, which were sharp. *Good lord!* She swallowed, trying hard not to panic. It was like being in the line of sight of a lion. Poised, ready and hungry.

"Where are my manners? This is my female, Page. Page, this is my brother, Obsidian. I told you about him."

Obsidian grunted.

"Um… I didn't know that… um… your brother is a twin." She tried to smile but only succeeded in grimacing "Hello," she squeaked.

Obsidian growled, more teeth flashed.

She sank down a little more in the water.

"Earth dragons only birth twins, and on rare occasions, multiples," Mountain said, it sounded like he was closer. "Even our human mates have all had twin pregnancies. I assumed you knew that."

She shook her head. Obsidian seemed to be calming down. His focus was no longer so unwavering, nor his muscles so bunched. *Thank goodness!* She could almost breathe again.

"It seems that slayers are not as informed as I would

have thought." Mountain looked like he was thinking about it. "That is a good thing."

"I only know what was conveyed to me. I wasn't—"

"Slayer," Obsidian snarled, looking at her like he wanted to kill her.

She shrank back into the tub, like the water might act as a barrier or something. Then Mountain was bowling his brother over. The two guys went down in a tangle of limbs and a cacophony of snarls and grunts.

There was a knock at the door. Then someone was entering. "What the hell!?" a male voice shouted. There was a loud clunk.

Page couldn't move. She didn't dare. She couldn't do anything, for fear of exposing herself to what felt like a room full of men. Even worse, the soap suds were dissipating. It wouldn't be long and there wouldn't be any left. She covered herself as best she could, praying they would all go away.

Mountain and Obsidian were rolling around on the floor, grunting and snarling up a storm. It was more of a wrestling match than a fist fight. They were so evenly matched. First one would be on top and then the other.

"Stop that!" the newcomer shouted. "Mountain! Obsidian! Stop." She caught a glimpse. It was Shale. He was trying to break up the fight. It wasn't working so he turned to her and grinned, giving her a wink. "They're like Neanderthals."

"Please just go away!" she yelled. "All of you!"

"Are you okay?" Shale asked, coming over to her.

"Stop!" she snapped. "Don't come any closer."

"Oh!" He raised his brows. "I get it. You're in the tub, so naked?" His brows went up even higher. "You don't have to worry, I've seen plenty of naked females."

What was it with these guys?

She squeezed her eyes shut and hunkered down as much as she could. By now there were no more bubbles left in the tub. The soap was still in her hand. Why had she grabbed it? Soap. The silent killer of bubbles everywhere.

"Get out!" Mountain roared, jumping to his feet. "Both of you," he added, looking at Obsidian who lumbered up to his feet as well. "Shale, I swear to fucking god, I will gouge your eyes out if you so much as see a half an inch of my female's flesh." Mountain pointed at Shale.

He chuckled. "You really are completely head over heels. You're smitten. Totally fucked." He laughed harder.

"Out! You too!" Mountain raged at Obsidian. "Use the door next time, or else."

Obsidian said something she couldn't make out.

"I appreciate you dropping by," Mountain said, sounding frustrated. "Thing is, I'm not alone, Obsidian. Thank you for caring, but—"

"Yeah," Obsidian grunted out the word, "I'll leave." He sounded gruff. Hardly even human. Then the door to the balcony was slamming.

"I'll see you later!" Mountain yelled. Then he was back at the tub, his muscles roping. His ass was sculpted and gorgeous. The towel, long gone. "I suggest you turn around, Shale. Leaving would be safer for you." He put himself between Shale and Page.

"Easy, big guy." She could hear that Shale was still smiling. "Your brother is getting worse. One of these days he won't be able to shift into his human form anymore. Can he even have a normal conversation?"

"Obsidian is fine!"

"That was not fine." Shale had an edge to his voice. His carefree attitude gone for once.

"He is," she could hear how angry Mountain sounded, "fine! I will—"

"Okay! Chill!" Shale said. "I'll take your word for it. I'm not here to discuss Obsidian with you. I have good news! The female—"

"Page," Mountain rasped. "My female has a name. Use it!"

"I can't believe how touchy you are about her. It's hilarious," Shale chuckled.

"Keep talking and you'll end up bleeding." Mountain fisted his hands at his sides.

"Relax. I brought your food and have good news for you guys. We can go and talk over there if it will make you feel better. I can't see your female's body if that's what you are worried about."

Mountain relaxed just a smidgen. She saw the tension ease from his shoulders. "Tell me and then leave." He began to walk away from the tub.

"It wasn't easy, I can tell you that much. Not easy at all, but I managed to convince Blaze to let you keep the female for your allotted two weeks. You can keep… Page, but you have to claim her today. You will have to continue to guard her and ensure that—"

Page didn't hear any more.

Claim.

As in sex. That's what claim meant. They needed to have sex today. She licked her lips and pushed out a silent breath. How did she feel about that?

Page smiled. Excited. That's how she felt. Blood rushed through her veins at the thought of it. *Yes!* She definitely wanted to have sex with Mountain. No doubt about it.

CHAPTER 13

There was no way he was having sex with Page. Not today at any rate. Hopefully soon. He hoped like hell it would happen soon. *Please god!*

"Enjoy, buddy!" Shale patted him on the arm. "You lucky fuck!" his friend added, his eyes moved to the ceiling for a second or two. "Although, I could do without all the commitment and just go with a good old-fashioned rut." He slapped Mountain a second time, grinning broadly. "I can see you don't agree."

That was very astute of Shale because the opposite was, indeed, true. He wanted the commitment. Wanted all of it. What he didn't want was to end up being a rebound relationship.

"Stop thinking so hard. Just do it! I'll see you later," Shale said. Mountain watched him walk down the hall. He went back into his chamber and closed the door. When he turned, his female was already out of the bath. She was wearing his t-shirt. It was very baggy and came down to her knees, but he was sure he had never seen anything more beautiful. The cotton clung to her damp curves. She was drying her hair with the towel.

"I'm sorry about that," he said.

She put the towel over the edge of the bath and began to finger brush her hair. He could hear the last of the water disappearing down the drain.

"Not your fault. You could have warned me though. What if I'd groped him by accident, thinking it was you? He's your identical twin brother. I can't believe that." She sounded exasperated. Her eyes were wide. "We both have a twin. What are the odds?"

Mountain shrugged. "I thought you knew. Like I said earlier, it's a simple fact about Earth dragons."

"I had no idea that your brother would be identical. That Earth dragons have multiples." She made a face of shock.

"I'm sorry. I would have said something otherwise."

"He does look exactly like you. Well... mostly." She smiled.

"Don't you dare go there." Mountain couldn't help but smile back.

She rolled her eyes. "I wasn't going to go anywhere. I happen to like your," she glanced down, "member exactly the way it is."

He put his hand over his semi-erection, feeling that familiar sense of insecurity. It had been a long while since he had experienced the emotion.

"You have the biggest... well," she giggled, putting a hand over her mouth, "almost the biggest cock I've ever seen and absolutely nothing to be ashamed about."

"Yeah, yeah," he clenched his jaw, "Obsidian beats me out, hence all the jokes about me having small dick syndrome." He chuckled. "I think I did suffer from it at one time."

Her mouth fell open for a second, but she quickly recovered. "Really? You? You have nothing to feel even remotely worried about." She walked over to him. That shirt looked so fucking good on her. *His* shirt. She went onto tiptoes and hooked her hands around his neck. "In fact, I think any more…" She looked down between them. At his cock, which was hard and jutting. She swallowed hard. "Any bigger than that and we may have had a problem. You are plenty big enough."

Mountain groaned, her eyes had turned greedy and she licked her lips. Page was talking about rutting. About them rutting. "About that. I—"

"I know. I understand what claiming is and," she smiled at him, sexy as sin, "I'm okay with it. I'd like to have sex with you. You said you could show me… more, and I want to feel… want to know more. With you."

He rubbed his hands up and down her sides. "I want to. More than anything. I can't wait to be inside you, to—"

"Okay then…" She smiled, stepping away from him and gripping the bottom of her shirt.

"No." He took her hands, stilling her. He let her go.

"Oh." Her blue eyes widened. "Oh shit! Of course. You must be starving after running for all those hours, and tired too. Exhausted."

"That's not it. I would love to fuck you…" He shook his head. "No, that's not true."

She frowned hard. "You don't want to," she paused, pulling in a breath, "to have sex with me? I thought that—"

"I do! I'm so damned attracted to you. I want inside you more than I've ever wanted it before, but I want it to be more than just fucking."

She frowned even harder. "What do you mean? That's what claiming means, right? It means having sex, doesn't it? Or am I missing something?"

"I…" *Shit!* How did he explain this without scaring her off? Mountain paced away from her as he gathered his thoughts. He turned and walked back. "I like you, Page."

Her lips curled into the start of a smile. "I like you too."

"I enjoy spending time with you. I think you are beautiful…" His eyes dipped down to her breasts, her tight nipples trying to poke holes through his shirt. At how full they looked under the baggy fabric. He so wanted to rip the shirt off her. His gaze dipped to her legs. Long, shapely, lush. "No, I like you a lot." He looked back into her beautiful eyes. "We haven't known each other very long but I know we could be good together. I know that already. I feel it." He put his hand to his chest. "Here."

"Oh." She sounded unsure. "That is soon."

"I wasn't talking shit when I told Granite that I had feelings for you."

"I see." She worried her bottom lip, something she did when she was thinking.

"I know this is more than likely a rebound relationship for you. Maybe even a way to… get back at your ex. Or to," he shrugged, feeling a pang, "even out things between you. He fucks around. You fuck around."

"No!" She sounded pissed. "That's not it at all. I don't fuck around." She looked pissed as well. "I told you, I've only ever had one partner and that's Shaun." Now she looked upset. "I wouldn't do that."

"I don't mean it like that." He tried again. "It wouldn't be intentional. I don't want to screw things up between us. I don't want to get hurt either, Page. There, I said it."

"You want more out of this?"

"Definitely," he answered quickly, "and you can't be sure about what you want at this point."

She shook her head. "I'm sorry. It's just that it's too soon. We hardly know each other, Mountain."

"I know what I want. You see, this has never been about anything other than finding a mate for me."

"What?" Her eyes were wide, her chest heaved. "What do you mean?"

"When I set out a few days ago, it was on a hunt. Human females signed up to take part."

"Why humans?"

"Sheesh! You really are out of the loop."

She smiled. "I'm not a slayer."

"Not a chance!" He smiled back, but he quickly turned serious again, as did she. "We don't have enough females of our own. That's why we've had to take human females. We're compatible as a species. We started off kidnapping females who met a certain… criteria, and then set about trying to convince them to accept us. It didn't work out all that well."

"I can imagine." She huffed out a breath.

"There are so many of us males and so few females that, about a century ago, we devised something called a hunt. The females have a head start and the males track behind them. We are not permitted to kill one another but there are many casualties along the way. Strength, stamina, agility, tracking skills, intelligence and then a good dose of communication skills are tested. Once a male captures a female, he must still convince her to mate with him, or it will all have been for nothing. He has two weeks to do so."

She looked shocked when he gave the timeframe.

He shrugged. "I was on a hunt the day I found you. I set out that day expecting to win a female."

"You sound so sure."

"Without being arrogant, I am one hundred percent sure I would have been successful in my endeavors. Unbeknown to me, the hunt was called off. It happened when you crashed."

"When I was fire-balled?"

"Yes. I am telling you all of this so that you can understand my mindset on this. My mindset in general. I set off that morning expecting to find the female I was going to spend my life with. I think you were running away from your life."

"No, I…" She stopped. He could see that she was deep in thought.

"I'm not saying you weren't… aren't trying to find your sister. All I'm saying is that there was more behind it. You'd caught your ex with another female just the day before. You were running. Might still be running."

"Maybe you're right." She nodded a couple of times, still in thought.

"We are in two different places in our lives. I think that throwing sex into the equation would complicate things."

She nodded once. He was happy to see that she looked disappointed. It was a step in the right direction.

"Let's get back onto human soil and find your sister."

Her eyes brightened. "That's a fantastic idea. I would be able to rest more easily knowing she is okay."

"You can already rest a little easier. It sounds like Beck is with her. He is highly skilled. If anyone can keep her safe, it's him. From what I have heard, she is highly skilled herself. The two of them must make a formidable team."

"And what then?"

"Then you need to go back to your old life."

Her shoulders slumped. Page didn't look like she relished the idea, which made him want to fist-pump the air.

"You need to see your ex and clear things up. Maybe," he swallowed hard, "you still have feelings for him."

Page didn't say anything. *Fuck!* He'd hoped she'd tell him he was wrong. That it wasn't true, but it never came.

"Right now, you are running, Page. Thing is, I want you running towards me, not away from something else that just happens to take you in my direction."

"You're right." She licked her lips. "About all of it. Okay, so we eat, get some rest and then we head out?" She raised her brows in question, looking at him expectantly.

Mountain cleared his throat. "There's just the pesky business of making it look like I've claimed you, without actually claiming you."

"Oh yes!" she sighed. "That's true. How do we do that? What will they look for?"

"My scent will need to be on you."

"That's easy." Page waved a hand. "We'll sleep in the same bed. I mean," her eyes widened, "that's if you're okay with that?"

"Of course. I don't want things to become awkward between us. I'm afraid that sleeping next to each other wouldn't be enough though." *Not even close.*

"We could spoon." She raised her brows.

He pushed out a laugh. "Still not nearly enough." He shook his head. "Although spooning sounds great."

"Oh, not enough huh?" She narrowed her eyes in thought. "We would need to make it seem like we had sex but without actually having sex?" She raised her brows.

"Yep, that's right."

"How do we do that?"

"I need to get my scent all over you. Look, I would understand if it's not what you want. I'll have a team of males escort you back to your home." He shook his head, running a hand through his wet hair. "I doubt Granite would allow me to take you myself. If I don't claim you, I can't stay with you. This will need to end. It will be up to you, but—"

"I was ready to have sex with you. I understand where you're coming from and you're right, I'm not ready for a relationship. Although Shaun and I are broken up, things between us haven't... they haven't been resolved. I'm almost a hundred percent sure it's over." She looked solemn. Her eyes were locked with his. "I'm pretty sure I want to explore this thing between us."

"Almost? Pretty sure?" He swallowed down his disappointment.

She winced and then smiled. "I need to see him. It's the only way I'll know for sure and even then," she shrugged, "I can't say I'll know exactly how I feel." She took his hand. "All I know is that I enjoy being with you. I like you very much. There could be more there. I just... I..." Another shrug. "It's confusing. There's too much going on."

"It's okay." He meant it. He could understand where she was coming from. She'd come to the dragon lands to find her sister. This was never meant to happen.

"What I'm trying to say is, I want to keep exploring this. I understand about the sex. I get it, but I don't want this to be over. I'm not ready for a relationship but I'm not ready to walk away either." He watched as her throat worked. "Let's do this claiming thing. I can tell you have something in mind. How do you plan on getting your scent on me?"

He pushed out a breath through his nose.

"Just tell me already."

Mountain swiped a hand over his face. "I need to come on you multiple times."

CHAPTER 14

He expected shock, which he got. Even though it lasted all of a second. Then he expected horror. Maybe a flinch, or an outright *'no.'*

He never expected the slow smile or the scent of arousal. This female was something else. "You're okay with that?" He had half expected her to tell him to go to hell.

"Yes." She nodded. "I'm fine with it. I had a feeling it would be something along those lines. Multiple times though?"

He nodded. "Yep. You up for that?"

More arousal and a nod. "I think I might owe you after…" Her cheeks flushed.

"You don't owe me anything. You're not going to do any of the work either." Mountain meant it.

She pulled in a sharp breath. "How are you going to… you know… if I don't help out?"

"We should probably eat first."

She nodded, folding some hair behind her ear.

He gestured to where a big tray was sitting on the table next to the main door. "Shale brought it just now, when Obsidian was here." He was seriously worried about the male.

"Oh, so that was the loud clunk I heard after he came in."

"He threw down the tray when he saw my brother and me. You go take a seat." He pointed to the dining-room table.

Mountain placed the tray of food on the table. There was a garden salad. Mashed potatoes, gravy and a couple of huge steaks. "Those are the biggest steaks I've ever seen."

"Elk steak," Mountain said. "Here." He put down a plate with a serrated steak knife and a fork. Then he placed one of the sodas from the tray, in front of her plate, and did the same for himself. Mountain put a couple of napkins on the table. Then he went to his closet and pulled on a fresh pair of pants. Loving how her eyes tracked his every move.

"I'm so hungry." She opened her soda and took a big gulp. "I hadn't realized until now," she said as he returned to the table, taking a seat.

"Yeah, me too." He sat down next to her and for the next while they dished and ate in silence.

"Your brother is nothing like you," Page finally said as she put her knife and fork down, half a steak still on her plate.

Mountain felt a pang. "He's never been very social, but he was never this bad either. I'm not sure why but he's slowly become worse over the last few years." He ate the piece that was on his fork.

"For a little while there I thought he might... hurt me." She licked her lips.

"I don't think so." Mountain shook his head. "He's ultimately a good male. Obsidian once told me that he thought people talked too much and that what they say is mostly unnecessary. He said that was why he preferred his scales. Being around people makes his head hurt."

"So, he likes to just be alone?" She shrugged, putting her napkin on the table next to her plate.

"I don't think so." Mountain cut another slice off his steak. "I've caught him staring at the she-dragons. Like he wants to approach them."

"Why doesn't he?" Page asked.

"It's not like he hasn't tried. They won't have anything to do with most of the males. There aren't many of them, so they can be picky about who they spend time with. He used to try to talk to one from time to time but was cut off at the knees. They were nasty about it too. I stay away from them now."

"Now?' She gave him a half-smile.

"I haven't been with a she-dragon in a very long time." He smiled back. "I prefer being with females who actually want to be with me. Females who..." He shrugged, trying to come up with the right words.

"Females? As in more than one?" She pretended to be offended.

He snorted out a laugh. "No, smartass, I'm a one-female kind of guy."

She smiled, looking sad for a moment. "I'm a one-guy kind of girl, although you would never say it."

"You're broken up, and we're not even having sex. Not really." He shook his head. "Stop giving yourself such a hard time."

"I know, and I know you are – a one-woman guy that is. What about a human woman for Obsidian? If you ask me, he's lonely. A woman would help bring him out of his shell."

"Are you serious? You met him. He leans a little more towards his animal side. Okay, a lot more towards that side. He would scare a human. He's banned from taking part in the Stag Run, as well as from participating in the hunt." Mountain felt guilty. "He tried to enter this last time round. Granite wouldn't hear of it."

"Poor thing! I'm sure he just needs the right person in his life."

"Poor thing?" Mountain chuckled. "You are making him out to be a puppy dog."

"He's no puppy dog, just misunderstood maybe?"

"Yeah, definitely misunderstood." His heart squeezed. Page seemed to understand, even though she didn't even know Obsidian. "I don't think there is a female out there capable of taming him. I will spend more time with him when we get back." *Shit!* '*We.*' He had said we instead of 'I.' A big assumption. "I need to try to reach him," he continued, hoping she hadn't noticed. "Like I said, there is a good male in there somewhere. I know it."

"You sound like me right now, defending my own sister. It's weird how we have more than one thing in common."

Mountain wiped his mouth, putting the napkin on his now empty plate. "Not so weird." He reached over and took her hand.

She blushed. "I guess."

He kissed her hand. "Are you tired?"

"I should be."

"Does that mean you're not?" His heart thumped faster.

Page's cheeks turned a rosy red. "Shall we do this thing? I mean, unless you're tired? You're the one who ran for hours with me on your back."

"I'm not tired at all." He traced a finger down the inside of her wrist, watching as her pupils dilated. It was back. Her arousal was in full force. He could practically taste it on his tongue.

"I think I might still be a little hungry." She bobbed her brows.

"You still have steak," he teased.

"Who's the smart-ass now? I'm hungry but not for elk, I'm hungry for dragon." She pushed her chair back.

"Oh, really now." He pushed his back as well.

"Oh, yes. When you talked about coming on me… would my mouth be a good place to start?"

Mountain closed his eyes and groaned. "I think that might be a perfect place."

"Good." She dropped to her knees right there in front of him. "At the table?" he asked, quirking a brow.

"Why not?" She bit down on her lower lip as she pulled the t-shirt over her head. Page was incredibly sexy. His dick hardened up to the point of pain and his balls pulled tight.

Then he had a thought. *Why now? Fuck!* Mountain didn't want her doing this because she felt she had to, or because she felt she owed him. Mountain cupped her jaw. "You don't have to do this. I could speak with Granite. I don't want you doing this because you feel some sort of duty…" He stopped talking when she narrowed her eyes.

"I want to be here. Duty?" She snorted. "Hardly! I will admit that... sex with Shaun felt like a chore. Whereas this doesn't... not at all." She rolled her eyes. "I really didn't want to bring him up. Not right now. I don't want to have a conversation about him. Save to say that I don't feel that with you." She smiled, looking so beautiful he felt the air catch in his lungs. "I want to give you pleasure. I want this." She licked her lips as her gaze dipped back to his cock.

"Okay then," he managed to grind out. His voice had dropped about a hundred octaves.

"Okay then." She gripped the elasticated band of his pants.

Mountain lifted his ass and she pulled them down. His cock sprang free, slapping against his stomach. He pulled them all the way down, stepping out of them. Mountain opened his legs for her.

Page moved in. "Ooooh! Someone wants this." She giggled.

"You have no fucking idea." He shook his head, watching as she leaned in closer and closer. "I have a feeling I'm not going to last very long," he rasped. "Don't judge me based on—" He groaned long and deep as her mouth closed over him. "Holy shit," he growled as she sucked him down. As her hand fisted his cock.

His hips jerked forward, and he held his breath. Her lips were wrapped so sweetly around his girth. Up and down, his cock hit the back of her throat and he jerked again. "Shit!" he rasped, trying hard to hold on.

His balls were posed for explosion... already. Then again, he'd been on edge for days. Ever since seeing this female for the first time.

She swirled her tongue over his tip, those gorgeous eyes of hers moving up to meet his. Although her mouth was solidly around him, he could have sworn the edges of her mouth turned up in a smile.

He could just imagine what she was seeing. His eyes would be wild... maybe a touch panicked since he was about to come and in under a minute. She'd never want sex with him after that. No fucking way! A male who couldn't go the distance. Best he hold on a little longer. Even if it killed him... and it just might. He was sweating. He could feel it gather on his brow. His teeth were clenched. He held the arms of the chair so as not to grab her hair and all-out fuck her mouth. Couldn't do that.

Couldn't!

Even though that was what she had done to him. Boy, had she ever. He thought about the sounds she had made. About how her pussy had spasmed. He couldn't wait to have her in that way. To make her come with his dick. He couldn't—

"Fuck!" he groaned. Shouldn't have pictured her coming. Shouldn't have imagined how her pussy would feel. Telling her he was about to come would have been the gentlemanly thing to do. He had planned on letting her know. On giving her the option of pulling away.

No such luck!

He groaned her name as he let go. *Let go? Nope.* Not the right description. Forget letting go. He was pushed over the edge. Free-falling had never felt so fucking good. His cock went off like a cannon.

Her eyes widened but she kept working him with her mouth and her hand. *Oh, that hand.* Putting everything into it. Her eyes on him. Filled with lust. Page swallowed him down as he shot off. He watched her throat work.

Swallow.

Swallow.

Swallow.

He grunted and groaned and grunted some more, sounding like a rabid animal. At one point his eyes rolled back. At least, that must have been what happened because everything went black. Maybe he passed out from the sheer, intense pleasure? It took a long while, but he finally came down. He let go of the armrest and it clattered to the ground. Broken. He'd ripped it clean off. "What the—?" His voice was guttural.

Page giggled. "I'm so glad you weren't holding the back of my head, or my neck or something. I could have died."

"Me too," he groaned. "You have one hell of a mouth, sweetheart."

"You're still hard." She was eyeing him like he was candy and she had a sweet tooth.

Mountain nodded. "It may not have seemed like it just now," he grinned, "but dragons usually have stamina. We can go multiple times." He winked at her.

"You're one big tease." She gave him a disapproving look.

Mountain could scent her arousal. "You didn't think I was going to leave you hanging, did you? That's not my style." He picked her up and began walking to the bed. "I need your scent on me too."

She leaned in and kissed him. Her lips soft. He could scent himself on her. He liked it. Liked it a little too much. He would be hurt if she decided to go back to her ex. It didn't matter that they hadn't had sex. He had feelings for Page and they were growing by the minute.

Mountain lay her down on his bed. He moved between her legs, loving her cry of pleasure as he laved her clit. He had a feeling it might be a while before they went to sleep, despite the long night they had just endured. Some things were far more important.

CHAPTER 15

The next day…

Granite's nostrils flared as he entered the male's office. His eyes narrowed just a smidgen and his nostrils flared a second time.

Stay cool!

Stay calm!

The fact of the matter was that they hadn't had sex. He may have Page's scent all over him. The opposite was also true, but they hadn't actually done the deed. Maybe Granite would pick up on that.

Stay calm!

His king might suspect, but he wouldn't be able to tell for sure. He couldn't let his actions give him away. He refused.

Mountain turned to the second male in the room and was shocked to see the Water king standing there. "My lord." He inclined his head.

"You know Torrent," Granite said. "Introductions

aren't necessary. I was just explaining to Torrent how you recently claimed Page. The slayer's sister."

"We're not sure that Alex is a slayer," Mountain pointed out. "In fact, I am convinced that she is not a slayer. My female seems sure as well."

"Not you too." Torrent frowned. "You fell for this female's bullshit? First Beck and now you too?"

That made his blood boil. Mountain waited a few beats, trying to clear his head, trying to slow his heart and to stop his adrenaline from pumping. Punching a king in the face wouldn't be a good idea, even if he was sorely tempted.

"You still need to prove without a doubt that your female is who she says she is. That she is innocent." Granite walked over to the window and stared out over the ocean in the distance. He turned back to face them. "It will be up to you to prove her innocence. I won't allow you to mate her otherwise. Until then, you are to guard her. Check out her story. If you find that she is lying, you need to bring her back to be dealt with."

"I can't." His blood still rushed through his veins. It still felt heated. If he wasn't careful, smoke would begin to filter from his mouth and nose. A dead giveaway.

"Can't what?" Granite asked, his jaw tightening. His eyes hard and unyielding.

"I…" He realized he was being stupid arguing with the male. Mountain believed Page was innocent. He believed it wholeheartedly. "I agree to guard my female. I agree to proving her innocence." It would be easy to do so.

"Do you also agree to bring her in if she is lying?" Granite's dark eyes seemed to darken further.

"It won't be necessary because she is exactly who she says she is."

"Mountain," Granite barked. "I want you to swear it."

"I swear," he finally rasped.

Granite pushed out a breath and nodded. "Good."

"You reported yesterday evening that you plan to seek out Alex Bell and Beck," Torrent stated.

"Yes." Mountain nodded. He had a feeling he wasn't going to like what was to come.

"Be careful." Granite's voice lost some of its biting edge. Concern bled into his features. "This could be a trap. She already has Beck, possibly against his will. They could end up capturing you as well. Two different dragons. Two separate lairs. It would be very convenient."

"Beck is no idiot, and neither am I. I doubt very much that they have him. I will prove my female's innocence and I will look into Alex Bell with an open mind. Do you have the information I requested?"

Torrent nodded. "Don't let this fall into the wrong hands."

"I won't."

Torrent handed him a piece of paper. Mountain read the words written there and raised his brows.

"We came up with safe words that would be difficult to crack." Torrent cocked his head.

"You're telling me." Mountain walked over to the paper shredder and inserted the document. He watched as it came out in ribbons on the other end.

"Please try to talk some sense into Beck," the male pleaded. "We will take him back, no questions asked. He needs to leave the female and—"

"With all due respect, my lord, I can't do that. Am I right in saying that Beck is your second in command?"

"Yes. At least he was until he betrayed his people for a

female. A slayer." Torrent looked stricken. "That female almost cost Tide his life. I don't understand how he could do this. Especially when Meghan has suffered from bad dreams and anxiety attacks." Alex Bell had shot Tide. She planned on abducting the royal pair when Beck intervened. He still couldn't believe that Beck would fall for a slayer. There had to be a reasonable explanation. Could it be that ten years later Alex Bell had still been clueless as to the real reason the organization existed? It had to be.

"I have met Beck on many occasions, and he is no fool."

"Love can blind a male. Lust too." He looked at Mountain like he was suffering from that exact fate.

"He is... *was* your second in command for a reason. You trusted him to lead. You trusted him to make split-second decisions, the right decisions even when faced with impossible choices. There is a reason you chose him for his role."

Torrent frowned. He looked like he was thinking it through.

"All I am saying is," Mountain looked at Granite and then back at Torrent, "I will not go into this blindly. I will not allow anything to cloud my judgment. Once I've established that all is above board, I plan on giving Beck the benefit of the doubt. He is in a relationship with Alex Bell. He may even have mated her by now. To ask him to leave her, to return... to leave his female..." Mountain shook his head. "I wouldn't do it, and so I won't ask it of him."

"Does that mean I won't see you again?" Granite sounded both upset and angry.

"You will see me again, my lord. I trust my female. I will bring her back and I will mate her." He hoped to god it ended up happening. They still had her ex to contend with. Maybe after all of that, she would still decide that she wanted to be alone. That she'd just come out of a bad relationship. It could be worse, she might go back to that prick. It could happen.

Granite pushed out a heavy breath, bringing him back from his thoughts. "I hope it all works out for your sake. Let us know if you need reinforcements."

"I will." Mountain turned to leave.

"Good luck," Torrent said.

Mountain glanced back. "Thank you." He hoped he wouldn't need it.

CHAPTER 16

Mountain drove the SUV while she inserted the SIM card into her new mobile phone. Her last one had died in the chopper crash. She fired the thing up. "Okay, so I take it I check out so far." She glanced at Mountain.

"I knew you would." He reached over and squeezed her thigh. "But I have to go through the motions. I hope you understand." He kept his eyes on the road ahead. "My king demands it. Make that, all of them do."

"You have to *guard* me until such time as you prove me completely innocent?" She laughed, still shocked. She'd been naïve enough to think that Granite was being nice. That guarding her would entail looking after her and keeping her safe. What Granite actually meant, Mountain later pointed out, was that he meant for Mountain to guard her so that she couldn't do harm to others.

"I apologized. I told you—"

"I know. It's fine. You can't control other people's thoughts or actions."

"But I *can* change their minds." He glanced her way

again, putting those gorgeous chestnut eyes on her.

She nodded. "One more stop and then I'm in the clear."

He put both hands back on the steering wheel. "Your apartment checked out. I just need to see your place of business." His Maps app blared in the background, directing him to Pencils and Things Stationers, where she'd spent every work day for the last seven years. She could hardly believe it had been that long.

Mountain needed to make sure that Erin Janet Blithe existed and that she and Page Bell were the same person. Were they the same person though? Were they really? Of course, physically they were, but otherwise she felt different as Page. More real. Stronger. Definitely stronger.

"The sales guy back there," she pointed behind them, "would not have given me a new SIM for my new phone if I wasn't Erin Blithe."

"I realize that." Mountain gave her a half-smile that did things to her. The man looked amazing in normal clothes. So far, she'd only seen him naked or in those cotton pants. He looked fantastic both ways, but decked out in jeans, a t-shirt... man oh man, but he was hot. There was something about a guy in jeans. Especially a big, muscular guy. She tried not to stare too much.

Not that the cotton pants had been bad. Thin and low-riding. She had a feeling he would look good in just about anything. A paper bag... a sack...

"We need to do it anyway. I need to report back to my king. I don't want anything standing in our way. I—" He clamped his mouth shut. "I want to keep our options open."

By options, he meant them, as a couple. Options for

them as a couple. Her stomach did this flip flop thing. It was both nerves and excitement. That was what was so darned frustrating. How could she be both scared shitless of something and really excited at the same time? "Okay. That's fine." She scrolled through her messages. There were a couple from Jenna. One from an insurance company hoping to sell her personal insurance for fifty percent less than what she was currently paying and... that was it.

Had she expected something from Shaun?

Was that it? Maybe she had. Especially considering the last time she had seen him he'd been with the lady from his work. Did she care that he hadn't bothered to text her again? No. It felt good that she didn't mind. Liberating even. That he hadn't called or texted spoke volumes.

Page sent a message to her friend, telling her she was okay, and then tossed the phone in her bag as they pulled up into her work parking lot.

"Wait a minute." Page pulled out her phone again and rechecked her messages. *Weird!* She scrolled through her emails as well. Double-checked everything.

"What is it?" Mountain frowned.

"I rented that helicopter. It was due back yesterday. They should have contacted me. They should have had an arrest warrant out on me by now. I have two missed calls, both of which are spam, and no messages or emails from the charter company. That's just plain odd."

"Don't worry about it."

"Of course I have to worry. I rented a helicopter and didn't return it. The chopper is a pile of ash and I don't have—"

"I sorted it out." Mountain turned in his seat to face

her.

"What? What do you mean by that? How did you sort it out?" She sounded skeptical.

"You said you rented the chopper… back when I first met you. I checked up on it when we got back to the lair. You were sleeping. I… I let them know that there had been an accident and I paid the company off."

She felt her jaw drop. "Um… I obviously have something wrong with my hearing. Did you say you paid for the helicopter I crashed?" She touched a hand to her chest.

He nodded. "A dragon fire-balled an unarmed craft out of the sky. The dragons need to cover your costs. It's the least we can do for almost killing you. I'm going to petition for further compensation, regardless of what happens between us."

"Further compensation?" She shook her head, feeling overwhelmed. "No, that wouldn't be necessary. I should never have entered restricted airspace. Private airspace. It was stupid of me." She thought back on his exact words. "You said *you* paid though. As in you personally? You footed the bill for an Airbus HC135?"

"It's not that big of a deal. I'll claim it back." He shrugged.

"That's big money." *Crazy money.* "That's… it's…" She pulled him into a hug. "Thank you." She breathed him in. He smelled of soap and of him. He smelled really good.

"Any time." He hugged her right back, wrapping her up tight.

She wished she could stay in his embrace all day or run away with him. Just the two of them. Somewhere remote and intimate. Somewhere where they served multi-colored drinks with little straws and umbrellas. Maybe one day. Maybe.

"It's pretty big," he said, staring ahead as she pulled back. Mountain pointed at the building in front of them.

"Not really, considering it's both the offices and the depot all in one."

"Still, how many pencils can one company sell?"

"You would be surprised," she smiled. "Pencils and Things supplies most of the schools around here with their annual stationary packs. We provide many of the local businesses with all their stationary needs and then there's the factory store – you can't see it from here, it's on the other side. I'll take you on a tour."

Mountain grinned at her. "We're wasting our time here." He put the SUV into reverse and shook his head. "I don't have to go in. I can tell you know this place like the back of your hand."

She put her hand over his. "No, let's go in. You said you need to go through the motions. That you need to be sure. Well, that means going in there." She pointed to the main doors. "I don't want you to have to guard me anymore."

"Maybe I like guarding you." He looked at her in a way that did things to her insides.

"Let's go in," she repeated. "We may as well, we're here already."

"You sure?" he asked; his cellphone beeped.

"Yes." She let go of his hand. "I'm still on vacation since I'm not due back until Monday. The story is, I left my driver's license in one of the drawers of my desk and I'm here to collect it."

"What about me?" Mountain gave her this look.

"You're my friend."

"Friend?" He scrubbed a hand over the light stubble on his jaw and then quirked up a brow.

"Yes." She snorted. "Men and women can be just friends you know?"

"Absolutely." He nodded once, like he didn't believe a word of it.

They got out of the car and headed for reception. Michelle smiled as soon as she saw Page. Her eyes widened when they landed on Mountain, who was looking at his phone. "Hey, Erin." Her eyes stayed glued on Mountain.

"Hi, Mich!"

"I didn't think you were due back till," she looked at her watch, "next week." Her eyes moved back to Mountain, who came and stood next to Page.

"I'm not officially back yet. I left something I needed at my desk, I'm just here to pick it up." That sounded believable.

"Who's your friend?"

Page smiled. See, men and women could totally be friends. "Oh, this is… this… I…" She couldn't call him Mountain. What kind of a human name was Mountain? It wasn't human at all. "Gary," she blurted. "This is my very good," *Cringe.* "friend, Gary."

"Hi, Gary, I'm Michelle. My friends call me Mich," She held out her hand, which Mountain shook. "I'm single," she added with a wink, still shaking Mountain's hand vigorously.

"Good to meet you. I'm here with Erin."

"Oh, yeah." Michelle let go. "Of course you are." She blushed profusely.

"See you shortly, Mich," Page said as they walked away. Michelle giggled like a schoolgirl.

Mountain laughed under his breath. "Gary? Did you just tell her that my name is Gary?" He laughed some more.

"Yes. What's wrong with that?" she whispered back.

"Nothing. Just that you're a terrible liar. You're not a slayer. You would never cut it as a slayer. Not in a million years. I'm not sure how you pulled off being Erin Blithe for so long without getting caught." He stopped walking.

She smiled, stopping as well. "That's the worst compliment anyone has ever paid me."

"It's not!" He put his hand to her back and smiled at her in a way that made her... well, it made her chest squeeze tight. "It's a straight-up compliment. You're not a liar. There's not a bad bone in your body. We're wasting our time here. Let's go and see your sister."

Her heart beat faster at the prospect. "Are you sure?"

"More sure than I've ever been about anything."

"Okay," she nodded. "Let's go and find Alex."

"I already know where she is," Mountain whispered. "I got a message from Beck a few minutes ago."

"What?" She felt her heart pound.

"I'm in the process of setting up a meeting."

"What are we waiting for?" She tried to keep her voice down.

Mountain nodded, and they headed back.

"That was quick," Michelle said as they entered the reception area.

"I knew exactly where it was." Page patted her bag as if her license was inside.

"See you next week then." Michelle waved.

Page waved back. The thought of having to return on Monday felt wrong somehow. It was hard to believe that she had still been working there less than a week ago. So much had changed. She only realized just how much now that she was back.

Then she saw who had just parked next to their SUV. Who was getting out of the silver BMW.

Oh no!

"That's Shaun's uncle," she whispered. "He's also my boss."

Sheldon did a double-take as he saw her. His brow furrowed. The lines around his mouth became more prominent for a few seconds. Then he smiled. "Erin. You're back early. Please tell me you're back?" He pushed out a dramatic sigh. "The temp isn't nearly as good as you. She doesn't get things done right. You know the way I like things to be done. The filing is a mess and—"

"Sorry, not yet. I'll be back Monday. I just needed to stop by to pick up my… something I needed. I… we'll be heading off now."

"Who is this?" Sheldon asked, narrowing his eyes on Mountain.

"This is Gary. Gary, this is my boss, Sheldon Jones. He owns Pencils and Things."

"Good to meet you. We'd better get going." Mountain opened the car door and stepped to the side.

Sheldon looked disapproving. "How do you know… Gary?"

It was none of his business, but she couldn't say that to his face. The man was her boss after all.

Page squared her shoulders. "Tinder, actually." She smiled. "I swiped right and the rest – as they say – is history." *Where had that come from?*

"Tinder?" Sheldon looked up at the sky, he frowned heavily. She could almost smell the smoke, that's how deep in thought he was.

"Shall we?" Mountain asked, gesturing inside the SUV.

"Yep, I think that's a good idea."

"Tinder," Sheldon said a second time. Then his eyes widened, and he pulled in a breath. "Oh!" he said almost to himself.

It was too late to take back. She might as well own it. Page smiled as she walked around to the passenger side of the vehicle to where Mountain was waiting.

"Wait a minute, Tinder... as in... I thought you were just on a break?" Sheldon asked. "Aren't you two getting back together?"

"It's not looking good I'm afraid." She shook her head "Goodbye," she said as she closed the door.

"What... why—?" he sputtered.

"I'll see you next week," Page added, just as she closed the door. She didn't want to get into it with him. It was none of Sheldon's business.

Mountain reversed out of the space. "You know he's going to call his nephew in a minute, don't you?"

"I don't care." Page was grinning.

"Okay then." Mountain smiled back. He didn't look as happy as she thought he would. It puzzled her.

"Where are we headed? Are we meeting with Alex now?"

Mountain nodded as they pulled out into the road. "They've agreed to come to us. We're going to an upmarket restaurant in town, so we'll need to stop at your place to change." He looked down at himself. "Collared shirts only and I doubt they'll accept jeans."

"Oh." She immediately began to panic. "I'm not sure I have anything suitable."

"You can go just like that." He threw her a smile.

"I'm in jeans. You just said that jeans wouldn't be allowed."

"On males, they wouldn't be. On you," he lifted his brows, "they'd let you in – in a hot minute."

She giggled. "That's sweet but misguided. I'm sure I have a black dress at the back of my closet." Her phone beeped and her bag vibrated. "Why all the fuss? I'm sure we can meet somewhere a little less fussy."

"We could, but I like the location. It's very public and has a rooftop – which means a quick escape if we need one."

"Do you still think Alex is guilty?" Page fished her phone out of her purse.

He shook his head, while indicating to turn. "No, I don't. I trust you, but it has been ten years since you saw her. I also," he raised his voice when she tried to interject, "I also trust Beck. It's just a precaution, that's all."

"Okay." She looked down at her phone and nearly dropped it.

> **Shaun:** Hey Honey, Hope you are well? I'm going to cut right to it. I miss you! Please call me so that we can set something up. A date maybe? Xxx

"It's him, isn't it?" Mountain asked, hands tightening on the wheel.

Fucking asshole! Crawling back. The dickhead had finally realized what he had, what he could lose, and was crawling back. Mountain couldn't blame him. He wondered why Page had told the uncle. She had to have known it would get back to her ex, and quickly. Had she done it to make Shaun jealous?

"Um," she licked her lips, "yes." She nodded. "It's Shaun. How did you know?"

"His uncle would have called him as soon as we left. I'm sure he had a lot to say."

"Yeah, but I didn't think it would change anything. A break is a break."

Mountain smiled even though he wasn't feeling particularly happy right then. In fact, he felt murderous. "The douche thought you would wait for him. He never in his wildest dreams thought you would... 'swipe right.'"

Her phone vibrated again. Of course it fucking did. Page hadn't texted him back immediately after reading his message.

She read the message, her throat working. *Great! Fucking awesome.* This is what he had been afraid of. That Page would go back to the jerk the moment she went back to her old life. Sometimes people just fell into old patterns. Old ways. It just happened. He hoped to god Page wasn't going to be one of those people.

"He... he—"

"You don't have to tell me." It was none of his business.

"It's bullshit." She shrugged.

Probably flowery crap. Or a declaration of love. Yup, now that he thought about it, it was probably that. There was another beep. "He's trying hard, isn't he?" More like blowing up her goddamned phone.

"He wants to meet," Page said.

"Of course he does," Mountain muttered, trying not to be a jerk about it.

Page shook her head. She dropped her phone back into her purse. "I'm not interested."

"You should meet him." Mountain wanted to chew his own tongue off for saying that.

"Why?"

"You need to be sure." He kept his eyes on the road ahead. "You need to look the male in the eyes and decide either way what you want to do."

"Because we won't be able to move forward otherwise?"

"It has nothing to do with us. You strike me as a reader, Page. Do you enjoy reading a good book?"

She nodded. "Yes, I do."

"Well, as a reader you should know that you can't skip pages. You definitely can't skip whole chapters. You can't skip to the end. It doesn't work like that. You have to read every page in order to understand where you are going and to fully comprehend the end."

"I didn't realize you were such a philosopher." He could hear she was smiling.

"I'm not. What I'm trying to say is that by not closing off that chapter in your life, you'll never know if that was what you were meant to do. Maybe you were meant to write more of this story and not close it." He was talking such shit but couldn't seem to stop. "You won't know for sure otherwise. You might regret things. You need to see him and go from there."

Page nodded, she looked like she was thinking it

through. "You're right. I mean, I had planned on seeing him all along, but now that I'm here…" She shrugged. "It's hard, that's all. It's harder than I thought it would be. I can do it though."

"You can," he said, watching as she pulled that damned phone out of her purse.

He forced himself to keep his eyes on the road. On negotiating the turns instead of watching Page read… and text.

Fuck! She was texting. Why had he said anything?

"I'm meeting him later this afternoon. Is that okay?"

No! He hated the idea. Fucking hated it. There was a part of him that hoped she was sure now. So sure she didn't need to see him. Thing was, Page wasn't that sure. He could hear the doubt in her voice and it was fucking killing him. "You don't have to ask my permission." He worked hard at sounding neutral. Thank claw, he managed.

"Oh." She made a face. "I know that, I wasn't asking," she paused, "I was checking to make sure we would be done with my sister and Beck."

"We're meeting them at noon." His voice had a rough edge, giving away his feelings some.

"You know what, I'm not going to want to cut our reunion short. I'll make it a breakfast… thing. Tomorrow." She texted while she spoke.

Thing.

What the fuck was a 'thing'? She could have said meeting or discussion or exe-fucking-cution. She could have just said breakfast even, but a 'thing'? Thing had an in-between sound to it. Like a meeting that could turn into a breakfast date, that could turn back into a relationship.

"You're grinding your teeth."

"I'm fine," he lied. "I'm just going through the plans for this afternoon." He parked in the guest parking bay at her apartment. "I need to guard you."

"Don't you mean them?" She smiled. "You're supposed to guard others from me, remember?"

"Oh, I'm pretty sure I plan on guarding you. I take it very seriously." Whether he was going to have to guard against slayers or her fucker of an ex, made no difference to him.

CHAPTER 17

"Stay here," he insisted. "Do not move from this spot."

"That's her. It's my sister." Page bit down on her lower lip. "Oh my god, she looks amazing." Her voice had a breathless edge. She sounded both in awe and excited.

The Water dragon held his female's hand. Alex was talking to him about colors. Random shit. Mountain was shocked at just how alike the two sisters were. Beck's gaze was on them. His eyes were also wide as he took in Page. He nodded, agreeing to whatever his female was saying. Beck grinned at him and squeezed his female's hand.

"Do not move," Mountain warned. "You know the plan."

"Yes, I do." Page was smiling broadly.

"Okay, I'll be right back," Mountain said. He was loath to leave her, but he had to. Beck was telling his female pretty much the same thing. The females spotted each other.

They strode to one another. Just like him, Beck looked

around the space. Checking. Taking it all in. "Fairy Butt." Beck grinned as he said it.

"That is the worst safe word I have ever heard." The safe word was used to ensure the person had not been compromised. Beck had already given it to him telephonically, and now, as a formality, he had delivered it correctly in person. Beck was right. It was a good one to have gone with. It was how Mountain had known they could meet without a problem.

"Come on," Beck's grin grew wider, "it's original. We were told to come up with something no one would ever think of saying in passing. Something no one else would be able to guess."

"Congratulations," Mountain said. "You did it." He gave a shocked gasp when Beck enveloped him in a hug. It was quick but solid. A man-hug at its best. One second they were hugging and the next they were apart again.

"I'm so happy to see you. I miss… home." His eyes grew misty. "You will need to tell me about everything I have missed."

"Alex." Page had moved in next to him. So much for staying put. Her throat worked.

"Page." Her sister's eyes filled with tears.

The females both made sobbing noises as they hugged.

He stayed alert, keeping an eye on the perimeter, as well as on the only entrance. The good news was, just as he had surmised, they would be able to make a quick exit in the case of an emergency. That would be a last resort though, since this was such a public location.

"I have to ask," Mountain said.

Beck's jaw tightened but he nodded once. "Go ahead."

"Are you sure your female isn't a slayer? Are you one

hundred percent positive?"

"Yes," his voice had a gruff edge, "she did work for the group causing all the shit, but she thought she was helping rather than hurting."

Page had already told him as much.

"Once we are seated, I can take you through all the events. Alex has proven to me that she is the person I know her to be. I—"

Mountain put his hand up. "Stop right there." He smiled at the male. "I trust your judgment."

Beck pushed out a breath. "Thank you." The male's eyes went back to the teary reunion.

Mountain couldn't help but smile watching the two females embrace. He felt a lump form in his throat. When he looked back over at Beck, he noticed that the male was smiling too. In fact, it looked as if his eyes were hazy, and he kept blinking.

Finally, Alex pulled away, giving Page the once-over, still clutching her sister's upper arms. They were both crying openly. "You look good," Alex sniffed.

"You do too." Page wiped under her eyes with the tips of her fingers.

"How have you been?"

"Good." Page sniffed. "You?"

"I'm good now. I thought you were dead." Alex made another sobbing noise.

"I'm sorry," Page whispered. "I'm so sorry," she added.

There was a waiter hovering around them. He looked unsure of what to do, given the emotional circumstances of the reunion. Mountain felt sorry for the poor male. "Shall we take our seats," he suggested.

The waiter sighed in obvious relief.

The females nodded, still smiling, still clutching one another and – much to the waiter's discomfort – still crying. He was all too happy to show them the way. It was a table on the balcony, right on the edge, away from the hustle and bustle, as requested.

Mountain put his hand to the small of Page's back. Beck took Alex's hand, smiling at her warmly. The male had clearly fallen hard for her, that much was evident. They scented heavily of one another.

The waiter ushered them to a table, helped the females take their seats and then handed Mountain the wine menu. Lastly, he took their drink orders and left.

"You are going to have to tell me all about the last ten years. What have you done? What have you seen? Where did you go?" Alex's eyes were animated. "How did you know? About Daddy and the organization, how did you find out? I want to know everything."

"It was Deborah who found out," Page said. She went on to fill Alex in, telling much the same story she had told him. Pausing when the waiter brought their drinks.

"I can't believe I was so blind." Alex shook her head. "I knew there must be something going on. Something that made you leave, but I chose to believe Daddy and for that I'm so sorry."

"I'm sorry I left you. I just…" Page wiped a tear away.

"No," Alex shook her head, "I wouldn't have listened. I know you tried. I was so set on proving myself. On winning back our father's affection even after…"

"He hurt you. He hurt us both," Page stammered.

It made Mountain's blood boil to hear of their pain.

"Yes, he did, and it's called brainwashing, Alex. You know that don't you?"

Alex nodded. "Yeah, I know."

"I keep telling her that." Beck put his arm around Alex. Alex's eyes softened as they landed on the male. She turned back to Page. "I mean, the way he used to lock you up…"

The waiter chose that moment to approach. "Have you decided on the appetizers?" He addressed Beck this time, then looked from one female to the other.

"Not yet," Mountain answered for everyone. "We haven't even looked at the menus yet."

"I'll give you a few more minutes then." He gave them a stiff smile before leaving.

"Let's put it behind us," Page said. "Let's focus on the here and the now and on the future."

"I agree." Alex smiled.

"What about you?" Page took a sip of her juice. "I know you stayed with the organization and that you recently escaped all of that. How are you coping?"

"I was lonely at first." She gave Beck a meaningful look.

"Not anymore," he said.

"Nope." Alex kept her eyes on Beck. "We've had quite an intense couple of days. It's been a rollercoaster. First…" Her eyes welled with tears. She flapped a hand in front of her face. "Sorry, I'm just so emotional." She gave Beck a watery smile. "I heard about the crash. I knew it was you who went down. Who else could it be? I grieved. I thought you were dead. I mean you don't just escape a helicopter crash."

"Yeah," Beck sighed. "I was told that a female matching Alex's description had crashed. I saw the site myself, there was nothing left of the chopper."

"I assumed the worst." Alex's lip quivered. "I thought

you were gone."

"I'm so sorry." Page grabbed her sister's hand. "It was such a stupid thing to do but I was desperate to find you. I heard you had escaped with your dragon." She glanced at Beck. "I heard about Harry. I was worried and not thinking clearly and I did a stupid thing. All I can say is that I'm grateful for all the training we had. All the tactical maneuvers. Learning how to skydive and base-jump. Otherwise, I wouldn't be alive right now, that's for sure. The dragon shifters don't like you much, by the way."

That elicited a growl from Beck which, in turn had a couple of diners from other tables looking their way.

"Easy," Mountain said. "We're going to clear things up with the kings. I had a long talk with Torrent, gave him some food for thought."

"Do you think they might accept me?" Alex raised her brows, her eyes brimmed with excitement.

"I told you." Beck clutched her hand. "It's not a risk I'm willing to take, not before and certainly not now. They'd question you. Lock you up." He growled again.

Alex nodded. "Okay," her eyes were on Beck's, "we don't have to rush into anything, we can—"

"Actually," Mountain interrupted. "I'm pretty sure it wouldn't take much to convince them. That was my biggest argument. They know *you*, Beck. They trust *you* and therefore, they will trust your judgment."

His eyes hardened and he shook his head. "I don't know, I just…" He made a sound of frustration. "I need her safe though, and out here," he shook his head, "on human territory," he looked around them, "there are pitfalls everywhere."

"You are not safe," Page agreed. "I've been in contact

with Debs, who has spies on the inside. From what I heard, Daddy was angry when you left. I think he was still hoping you would come around one day. That you'd accept his evil plans and work for the organization in a different capacity, with different agendas. You leaving like you did stung him. It lost him credibility with the other founding families. He is out for blood."

Beck ground his teeth so hard that Mountain was sure his molars might bleed.

Alex widened her eyes. "I know, I heard something similar."

"He half-heartedly tried to track me over the years, may have put some feelers out for me, but it's different where you are concerned," Page said, her eyes wide and filled with concern. "Deborah's sources say he appointed a special task team to hunt you down."

Alex bit down on her lip, looking so much like Page that it was uncanny. Her eyes filled with more tears. She tried to blink them back, but it didn't work. "I'm pregnant," she blurted.

Of course!

Shit! He had scented something off with her but hadn't been able to put his finger on it with so many other scents about. With Beck's scent all over her.

Page squealed. She covered her mouth with her hand, her eyes wide.

"I know," Alex whispered. "I was shocked to find out. I was on birth control. I get injected every six months, but I guess it's not foolproof."

Page got out of her chair so that she could hug her sister. "I'm so happy for you." She went and hugged Beck as well.

"Shifter seed is potent," Beck said under his breath, grinning broadly.

"You need to be careful." Alex winked at Page, who blushed, giving the tiniest of headshakes. "What?" Alex asked. "Oh…" she added under her breath, making a face. "Sorry. I just… I assumed… I—"

"Congratulations," Mountain interjected, forcing a grin. It was fantastic news after all. "On both the baby and your mating."

Beck's grin turned into an immediate frown. "No, we're… um… We're not mated."

"Why not?" Mountain felt himself frown right back.

Beck glanced at Alex. "It wasn't the right—"

"Beck wants nothing more than to mate me, and I feel the same." She pulled in a deep breath. "But I can't. Not when his people haven't accepted me. It doesn't feel right."

"Well, that settles it. You need to come back. It might be tricky at first, but once you talk to them… Tell them everything. They need the facts. Ultimately, they will trust *you*, Beck. Your female is with child. They will have to accept her."

"So you keep saying." The male looked sad. "I just can't take the risk though." He shook his head vehemently, but at the same time, Mountain could see he was thinking it through.

CHAPTER 18

It felt strange to step through the threshold. The tables were all in the same places they had always been. The pastries were lined up in the display cabinet. Page didn't have to look to know which ones were in there. It even smelled the same in here. Coffee, vanilla and freshly baked bread.

The barista waved at her from behind the coffee machine. "Hey, Erin. Good to see you."

For a split second, she wanted to turn and look behind her. Then she realized he was talking to her.

Erin.

Right.

She waved back, her arm feeling stiff, her smile forced. "Hi, Sid."

"Your usual?" he asked, poised to push a button on the machine.

"No, thanks. I'll order in a few."

Sid nodded and got back to wiping down the counter.

"You okay?" Mountain asked from behind her.

She realized that she was hovering in the doorway and stepped forward, glancing back at him. "All good." Her voice sounded bright and breezy. This was all going to be just fine and dandy.

"Good." His voice was clipped, his movements tense. His eyes were darker than normal. A direct correlation to his mood. Leaning more towards brown than that beautiful chestnut color she knew.

"Are you okay?" She touched his arm.

His jaw tensed up for a moment. "Yes. I will have a look around and then I'll wait in the car out front."

"You really don't have to…"

"I must," Mountain all but growled. "While I am on… here, I will protect you. I must do my duty."

Duty.

She nodded once, her chest tightening. Everything had changed yesterday after the texts from Shaun came through. It was like someone had stuck an invisible barrier between the two of them. There was this tension that hadn't been there before. At first, it wasn't as noticeable, she'd been buzzing with excitement to see Alex. Then they'd had a light supper once they got back to the apartment, though they'd barely spoken. Mountain had insisted on sleeping in the spare room. She tried to bring it up, but he'd cut her off. He had hardly said two words to her. Page couldn't blame him. This was a difficult situation.

"I know we had this discussion earlier," she said. "I lived here for years. I've been perfectly safe. I—"

"I'm staying. I'll keep out of your way. I'm not here to stop you. If you want to get back with your boyfriend, I won't stand in your way."

Why not?

Didn't he even want to try to fight for her? Suddenly Shaun was her boyfriend and not her ex. She felt like groaning in frustration or throwing something. Instead, she nodded once. "Whatever makes you happy."

He ground his teeth. "I'm going to do my checks. I might need to come back inside. If something looks suspicious or... if I need the restroom... ignore me. I'll stay out of your way."

The way he said that was almost final. *I'll stay out of your way.*

"Okay." Less bright and breezy, a little more high-pitched. His words stung. "Can I get you a coffee to go?"

Mountain shook his head. "I'll pick something up on the way out."

Page tried to smile but couldn't. Not when he was frowning so deeply. Not when he looked so angry. She wasn't sure why, since he was insisting that she do this. Now, suddenly, he seemed to have a problem with it. Thing was, she *did* need to face up to Shaun. This needed to happen. She watched him disappear behind a door that led to the restrooms.

Page took a seat close to the window as Mountain had instructed earlier. A few minutes later, he returned and bought himself a bottle of water. Not even looking her way as he left. She watched him get into the SUV, which was parked right in front of the coffee shop.

The minutes ticked by. Nine o'clock came and went. Maybe she should have ordered a drink.

Finally, she spotted Shaun. Ten minutes late. Typical. He grinned at her as he walked through the door. He walked straight over and hugged her, even though she stayed in her seat. Then he planted a kiss on the side of her mouth before she could react. *Unexpected.* "Good to see you, Erin."

Erin.

It felt odd to be called that again, which was silly. She'd been known as Erin for ten long years. You would think being called Page again would be odd, but it was the other way around.

Shaun didn't apologize, instead he headed for the counter and placed their order. A large, regular cappuccino for himself and a medium skinny for her. Then, he bought a sticky cinnamon bun and headed back, a smile plastered on his face. "Here you go." He placed the coffee in front of her and the bun between them. "Just like old times." He winked at her.

"Thank you."

"You look different." Shaun scrutinized her. "I can't put my finger on it. It's like you're glowing. You're…" His eyes widened. "That's it. You're not wearing your glasses."

"I'm trying out contacts," she lied, then shrugged. "Thought I'd do something different."

"Well, you look great. My uncle tells me that you're on vacation. What have you been doing? Did you go anywhere?" He scratched his right thigh, holding her gaze.

She shook her head. *What could she say? 'I headed into dragon lands, got shot from the sky and met a dragon shifter.'* "No, nothing much. I needed some time off. That's all."

"Okay, so you haven't done anything interesting?" He took a sip of his coffee, adjusting himself in his seat.

Shaun was alluding to Mountain. He was trying to get her to talk about him. Well, two could play at that game. "Nope. What about you? Any interesting news?"

"No," he made a snorting noise. "Same old." More squirming in his seat.

"And Daniella? Are the two of you dating? It would be okay if you were." She took a sip of her coffee. It tasted bland.

Shaun pulled a piece off the cinnamon bun before offering the pastry to her. She declined. "I told you, we're just work colleagues. It's not like that."

"We're technically broken up, Shaun. I wouldn't be upset. You might have dated other women, even slept with them." She raised her brows.

He squirmed some more, scratching his left thigh this time. "Nope! Not at all. My uncle tells me you're dating though." A nice change of subject. "You brought some guy to work yesterday. Quite frankly, I find that hard to believe." There was an edge to his voice she didn't like.

"Why is it so hard to believe?"

"I don't mean it like that. I mean, of course you're a gorgeous girl, with plenty to offer." He finally put the piece of pastry in his mouth. "I just can't believe you would... that you'd..." He spoke around his food.

"Move on?"

He looked shocked for a moment but quickly composed himself. "I asked you if you'd wait for me, Erin. I fully intended for us to get married. I still do."

"We also agreed we were broken up. Free to see other people. I don't see the problem."

"Yeah, but that was just a formality. I didn't screw around on you." His voice took on a nasal edge. "I needed a breather. Some time to focus on me. I didn't actually think you would start seeing someone else." He took a breath, tensed. "You *are* dating someone else right?" He shifted in his seat, looking uncomfortable.

"No, Shaun, I'm not dating anyone."

He visibly relaxed. His scowl turned to a grin. "Of course not." He threw out a laugh. "I should have known my uncle got it wrong. You would never pick some guy up off of Tinder. You wouldn't," he made a snorting sound, "do something so crazy. You're a good girl, Erin, you…" He got this look of discomfort. "I need to use the little boy's room." He looked at the door that led there. "I'll be back in a second." Shaun stood up. "We can discuss our future when I get back. I want my ring back on your finger. We need to set a date. Something soon." He bent at the knees a little, looking really uncomfortable. "I need to go. I shouldn't have had three cups of coffee this morning." He widened his eyes.

Page watched as he practically ran from the room. She glanced at the SUV, expecting to see Mountain, but he wasn't there.

What?

The door to the coffee shop opened and he sauntered in, looking murderous. He glanced at her as he headed for the restrooms.

"No." She shook her head. "Don't!" she said more forcefully, but Mountain didn't listen to her.

"Stay here," he instructed as he pushed the door.

"No! You can't…" she begged.

"I won't… do anything stupid." Then the door was closing behind him.

Holy crap!

Should she go in after them?

Oh god! Was Mountain going to kill Shaun?

No! He said he wasn't going to do anything stupid. That

wasn't a given though. Maybe he just needed to go to the bathroom.

Yeah, right!

She strained to hear… anything… something. There was no screaming. No crashing or bashing. No noise whatsoever. Maybe it would be okay. Page put the tips of her fingers to her temples and pushed. The next four minutes were the longest of her life.

CHAPTER 19

Mountain entered the bathroom. There were two urinals against the far wall and two stalls. He caught the strong smell of cleaning detergents. He could also scent the male, the smell pissed him the fuck off. One of the doors was closed. He heard what sounded like scratching and then a low moan. It was both a moan of pleasure and frustration. Then more scratching.

Odd!

What the fuck was the asshole doing in there?

He gave the stall door a hard shove, the flimsy mechanism broke, and the door opened with a crash, smashing the side of the stall.

The male sat on the toilet, jeans pulled around his ankles, he was vigorously scratching his balls, his face contorted in pain and pleasure. The male snatched his hand away and then fumbled with his pants. "What the— What the heck?" He sounded indignant. Hard done by.

Fucker!

Mountain could put two and two together about what

was going on in there. His nose told him everything else he needed to know.

"You need to listen, and you need to listen good," Mountain said, voice low.

"Who the fuck are you?" the prick said, as he tucked his pencil dick into his pants. His eyes brightened as he pulled up the zipper. "It's you... the asshole from Tinder. Gary," he said the name with a sneer. "My uncle described you. What the fuck are you doing here? Erin and I are in the process of getting back together, so you can turn around and leave. You're wasting your breath."

"Okay. No problem."

The prick's face scrunched up in confusion. "You're leaving?" He didn't sound sure.

"Yes, I'm leaving, and I won't pound your face into the floor if you do one simple thing."

The asshole gasped like a girl. He even put a hand to his chest.

"Just so we are very clear, if it was up to me, I would smash your nose into your face."

Shaun's mouth fell open.

"Did you know that the nose is made out of cartilage? Cartilage is softer than bone. It makes this beautiful crunching noise when it breaks."

The crybaby made a squeaking sound, his eyes growing wider by the second.

"It's quite possible to punch it flat." He smirked. "I could make it look like a bloody pancake on your face." Mountain couldn't hold back his grin, it quickly turned into a sneer though but only because of how badly he wanted to hurt the SOB.

The fucker put up both hands. "Please don't...

please…" His eyes filled with tears.

"I will leave. I will turn around and never look back if you guys decide to get back together. That will be fine with me." It would be so far from fine, but he'd deal. "I won't lay so much as a finger on you, but you need to come clean."

"Come clean about what?" His lip wobbled and he sounded panicked.

"You know what. You know exactly what I'm talking about."

He shook his head, shaking it so quickly it was comical. "I don't, I have no clue. I swear!"

"You may have been on a break. Not together as a couple, but I want you to tell… Erin…" It felt wrong calling her that. "I want you to tell Erin exactly what you were up to during your break."

"Erin dated you. She said you guys are finished, but she dated you. You can't tell me the two of you—?"

"I'm not going to tell you shit!" Mountain interrupted. "That's for Erin to discuss with you. For you to discuss with… with—" *Fuck!* "With your girlfriend." It hurt to say it. Page had said she and Mountain weren't dating though. It did look like she and this bozo were getting back together, but the fucker needed to be very honest first. Mountain knew Page would be. Just as he knew that if left alone, this fucker would lie through his teeth.

If Page decided she didn't want to be with Mountain, which it seemed like she had, it was fine. It fucking killed him, but it was her decision. She just needed to have all the facts before deciding how to proceed with this loser. "I know what you've been up to and I'll know if you don't come clean about all of it."

"All of it? How could you possibly—" His eyes were filled with shock.

"I just do!" Mountain bluffed. He knew enough, maybe not all, but enough. Mountain growled, taking a step forward.

The prick cowered in the back of the stall. "Please don't hurt me. Please."

"I won't, but if you don't come clean, all bets are off." He clicked his knuckles. "Plastic surgery wouldn't be enough to save it." He looked down at the asshole's nose.

The coward covered his face with his hand. "Okay! Okay! I'll tell her. Please, just don't," he whined.

"Don't try to bullshit me. I'm listening in and I'll be waiting for you if—"

"I said I would do it," the male sounded pathetic, "and I will! I swear it."

"Go then," Mountain moved out of his way.

The prick left the stall, heading for the door. "Wash your hands first," Mountain said.

"What?" He frowned.

"You heard me. Wash your hands." He grimaced. "And use soap."

Shaun walked out first. He looked fine. As in, there was no blood and no bruising. None that she could see, at any rate.

His face was ashen, and he was sweating profusely. Something had gone down in that bathroom. That much was very clear.

He leaned in and put his hands on the edge of the table. Tension radiated off of him. It didn't look like he planned on sitting down. His eyes were wide. Shaun glanced back over his shoulder, looking at the closed door for a few beats.

Then he looked her in the eyes and licked her lips. "I had sex with her," he finally said, between clenched teeth.

"What are you talking about?" she asked. "Who did you have sex with?"

"Daniella from work. I had sex with her. I had sex with her that same day you saw us. I've had sex with her every day since."

Page frowned. *What on earth?*

There was the sound of a door closing, it drew their attention. Shaun glanced back. Mountain stood in the door jamb, arms folded, a scowl on his face. "Jesus!" Shaun whimpered squeezing his eyes closed. He seemed to fold in on himself. His shoulders rounded. Sweat poured off of him. "Um... I... um... I had sex with her this morning before coming here," he whimpered. "I had planned on breaking up with her when we got back together. *If* we got back together. There! I said it!"

There was a soft growling from behind them.

Shaun choked out a sob. "Please don't let him hurt me." He sniffed loudly. "Oh, Jesus, please... um..." He sniffed, sobering up. His eyes glistened. "I had sex with two other women, during our break," he blurted.

"Other than Daniella?" she asked.

"Yes. Girls I picked up. One-night stands," he sobbed. "It didn't mean anything. I love you, Erin. Please, I want my ring back on your finger. Please don't let this be the end."

"You lied to me," she said. "I asked you straight out if you were seeing Daniella and you lied."

"You lied too." Shaun stood up straighter. "You fucked that guy." He waved a hand at Mountain.

"Yeah, so?" He didn't need to know that it technically wasn't true. Thing was, they may as well have slept together. At least, in her eyes.

"So, you lied too."

"No, I didn't. We didn't get that far in our discussion yet. I planned on telling you. You never asked me straight out though, Shaun. You asked if we were dating and I said that we weren't. Look, it doesn't matter anyway." She stood up, her chair scraping. "It's over between you and me."

"No, you can't be serious." He sounded shocked. Even after his admission, he still expected her to just bow down and accept him back. How had she put up with this for so many years?

"I am through, Shaun. It's done! It's over!" She picked up her purse.

"I'm so sorry!" He rubbed a hand over his face, his expression stricken. "I should never have slept with those girls. I should never—"

"Women."

He frowned. "What?"

"Women, they're women, not girls and quite frankly I feel sorry for them."

"Why would you say that?" He really was clueless.

"It would take me too long to explain, and I don't want to waste my time." Shaun wouldn't listen anyway. "Goodbye! Have a nice life."

"But, Erin, I—"

She ignored him. Mountain was already at the door, holding it open for her. She didn't look at him or thank him.

Page heard him follow her. They got into the SUV. Page buckled up as they pulled off. "You didn't have to do that, you know." *Shit!* She sounded angry.

"I did," Mountain growled, sounding angry as well. "I absolutely did. You do know that jerk wasn't going to tell you?"

"I don't care. I didn't need to know."

"You didn't need to know?" He did a double-take. "He lied to you. He has an STD. A sexually transmitted—"

"I know what an STD is," she countered.

"I could scent it on him. I caught him scratching his balls. Did you want to catch that from him?" Mountain's hands tightened on the wheel. "Is that it?"

"I wasn't going to catch anything from him because I wasn't ever going to stay with him."

"You could have…" Mountain stopped talking, realizing what she had just said. "You weren't going to make up?" He stopped at a red light.

"No! I can fight my own battles. I didn't need you to fight them for me."

"But the kiss. What was that about?" He glanced her way and then pulled off as the light turned green.

"That was him catching me unawares." She made a disgusted noise, feeling sick to her stomach. "I didn't expect it. Didn't want it. I need to scrub my face and singe my skin with scalding water."

"You were about to take back his ring." Mountain sounded hurt. His eyes looked wounded. His hands were tight on the wheel.

"I wasn't. I never agreed to any of what he was saying. He left to go and scratch his balls," she bit back a laugh, "before I could set him straight."

"You…" Mountain clenched his jaw for a moment. "You told him we weren't dating." They pulled into the parking at her apartment block. "I heard you say it clear as day. I guess you don't want either of us then? Do you need time? Or—"

"You shouldn't have been eavesdropping." She unbuckled her seatbelt.

"I couldn't help it, okay? I was going nuts in the car. Especially after that kiss."

"He barely even got my lips," she mumbled. "You shouldn't eavesdrop because sometimes, when you eavesdrop, you get the wrong end of the stick. That's what happened today."

"Wrong end of the stick. How could that be? You said we weren't dating. How can I have gotten that wrong? I heard you. He asked, you answered." He twisted around in his seat, looking at her head on.

"Are you done?"

Mountain took to looking sheepish. That, and concerned.

"I told Shaun that because you and I are way past dating, Mountain. I hardly know you. A part of me is freaking out right now because of that fact, but one thing I do know is that I love you. I want to be with you, not Shaun. Forget Shaun! You," she touched his shirt, "mean everything to me."

She watched his facial expression go from sorrow, to shock then to happiness in the space of a few seconds.

"You love me?" He narrowed his eyes. The corners of his mouth twitching

"Yes, I do." A whisper.

"I really thought you didn't want me. I thought you had decided to stay with him. I'm sorry, but I couldn't let that happen."

She pulled in a breath, getting ready to argue all over again.

"Before you say anything," he put up a hand, "I should have let you handle it. I should have known you would do the right thing in the end. I'm your guard. I'm here to protect you. My instincts to do just that may have taken over."

"I somehow doubt that getting Shaun to confess falls into the spectrum of duties." She raised her brows feeling skeptical.

"Screw my duties."

She couldn't help but grin at that admission.

"I don't give a shit about my duties. I care about you, Page." He cupped her chin, looking deep into her eyes. "I want to keep on protecting you. I want to be the protector of your heart. I want to love you and keep you safe, happy, content."

"Sold!" Page yelled, throwing her arms around his neck. "Can we please have sex now?"

Mountain grinned. "I would love to have sex." He closed his mouth over hers, deepening the kiss. Then he pulled back. "You have no idea how much I want sex." He took back her mouth.

Page pulled back. "No, I think I do."

Mountain leaned over and gripped her hips in his big hands and Page moaned. He smelled so good. Woodsy and earthy and soapy. He tasted even better... like Mountain, like hers.

Mine.

She smiled against his mouth. It was her turn to say it.

"What is it?" he asked.

"You're mine," she murmured.

"Yes, I am." He lifted her onto his lap, and she straddled him. She slid her arms around his neck and pushed herself against him. Mountain squeezed her breast, making her moan again, louder this time. He rubbed his thumb over her nipple, and she felt it harden. They kissed with an urgency she hadn't felt before.

Then his hand was between her legs, he rubbed her through her jeans. "Oh god," she moaned against his mouth, feeling need pulse through her.

Knock! Knock!

She pulled back, her mind feeling dull. What—?

"You can't... do that here," the security guard said, staring at them through the window. He was frowning heavily, looking unhappy.

"Oh shit!" she whispered, peeling herself off of Mountain.

"Sorry," Mountain stammered. She clambered back over onto her side of the car. Mountain opened his door.

"Extremely, sorry... it's Carl, right?" She peered over at the guard, her face feeling hot.

He nodded, still looking stern.

"We'll go inside now," Page quickly said as she got out of the vehicle.

"Best you do that." The guard looked from Page to Mountain and then back again. "I should have called the cops but that won't happen again, will it?" He looked at Mountain as he exited the vehicle as well.

"Oh, it most certainly will, but not in public," Mountain added, walking over to her side and shutting her car door for her. He locked the SUV and the alarm beep sounded.

"You guys just start dating?" Carl's expression softened.

"We're not dating," Mountain answered. "We just got engaged and it's going to be a *short* engagement. We may have gotten a little carried away." He winked at her.

Page felt her cheeks heat even more.

"I'll let this slide with a warning then." Carl smiled. "Congratulations on the engagement."

"Thank you," Mountain replied, taking her hand.

"We'll see you, Carl," she said over her shoulder as they began walking towards the apartment. She bit down on her lip to keep from laughing. Mountain had a naughty grin on his face.

"I always thought you could do better than that guy you were with," Carl called at their retreating backs, voice raised.

She glanced back, her smile growing by the second.

Mountain walked so quickly she had to jog a little to keep up. "We're engaged?" she asked as they arrived in the foyer.

Mountain turned to face her, his eyes stricken. "Shit! It's okay I said that, isn't it? Wait a sec," he added before she could say anything. He got down on his knees. It was heartwarming seeing such a big guy down on the floor in front of her.

She clutched her chest with one hand and held his with the other.

"I'll admit this isn't the most romantic way of proposing but please know it's from the heart. Will you mate with me Page Bell? We'll have a short engagement because I can't wait to make you mine… officially."

"Yes." She nodded. "I would love that."

"Good." He jumped to his feet and kissed her, his arms enveloping her. He pulled back. "We'll go ring shopping... later." He brushed his lips over hers, smiling.

"Much later," she said against his mouth. "But first—"

"Sex." His eyes practically glowed with excitement. He pushed the elevator button five times in quick succession.

Page laughed when he pushed on it another two times. The doors pinged as they opened. As soon as they closed behind them, Mountain had her up against the wall. He cupped her ass, hoisting her against him. He kissed her neck, nibbled on her ear. Then he kissed her mouth, deepening the kiss instantly, rubbing his hardness against her core. Making her lose her mind.

He pulled back and she almost fell on her face. Would have too if he didn't grip her elbow. The elevator door opened with another ding. They rushed down the hallway. This time at a jog. It took her a few seconds to find her keys and then they were in her apartment. His mouth on her. His hands on her. Her hands... all over him.

Page broke the kiss but only so that she could pull her shirt over her head. His eyes zoned in on her chest. He yanked his own shirt over his head and made quick work of his jeans while she pulled hers down her thighs.

She stepped out of her shoes and then her jeans, almost at the same time.

Mountain growled low, tugging at her bra. There was a ripping noise and her boobs popped free.

She made a sound of desperation as he picked her up. She put her legs around him, feeling him there, against her core. She'd never been crazy for sex before. She rubbed herself against him and Mountain's chest vibrated with a low groan of raw need. Clenching, puckering, aching. Lots of her parts were doing all three.

Then her ass was hitting something hard. Mountain flipped her onto her stomach. It was the table. Her boobs mashed against the hard surface. Her feet made contact with the ground.

"Open for me." There was a desperate edge to his voice, as he gripped her hips. He growled low when she did as he asked. "So pink," he moaned, sliding a finger into her.

She mewled. The noise tearing free and reverberating around her small apartment.

"So wet." He sounded like he was in awe. His voice was deep and animalistic. It did things to her.

Her eyes widened and she struggled to breathe as his finger moved in and out of her. His thumb found her clit, which he rubbed as well. She moaned, her hands splayed on the table. It was already so good. So unbelievably good.

Then he was gone. She made a noise of frustration, wanting more… so much more. Her eyes widened up when he put the thick head of his cock against her opening. At this point, Page was panting. He nudged her pussy, breaching her slowly.

Mountain groaned loudly as his head slid into her. God, but he was big. It stung a bit. She made a whimpering noise, trying hard not to tense against him.

"Keep breathing," he cautioned. "It will start to feel good in just a few seconds." His hand tightened on her hip.

"O-okay," she stammered. His finger found her clit again and he strummed it with firm, even strokes.

Her panting increased, becoming louder, laced with the

start of a moan.

Mountain nudged his way in using slow, easy strokes. Page moaned as he pushed deeper. It stung a little, but it also felt good. Mountain grunted hard as he bottomed out inside her. His hips were against her ass. His cock pulsed inside her. He crouched over her. "You feel amazing." It sounded like he was straining. "You ready?"

"Yes," she whimpered.

"Good," he growled as he slid almost free of her before thrusting back in… hard. Page yelled, but only because it felt so good. The table scraped against the floor, moving a little with each thrust.

Shit!

Shit!

It felt… it… it felt… amazing. He thrust again and there was another scrape. After a good few hard thrusts, the table thud against the wall where it anchored. Her yells and moans were loud, but she couldn't stop making them. He had one hand on her hip and the other on the table next to her. By the noises he was making, she could tell he was going to finish soon, which was okay. Perfectly fine.

Her mouth was wide open. Her eyes were fixed that way too… unblinking. Page could feel the coiling inside her. She could feel he was hitting a place inside her that was doing things… incredible things… *Oh god!* There was a chance she might make it there. Then again, his movements were so determined. She mustn't be disappointed if it didn't happen. Even though this was the closest she had ever come to having an actual orgasm during sex.

He grunted and groaned and grunted some more. His thrusts coming quicker now… more urgent. Her lower belly seemed to tighten.

Any second and he was going to start jerking and groaning. The crazy thing was that this would still be the best sex she had ever had. She felt him crouch a little lower over her, could feel his weight increase, could feel his heat down the length of her back. He kept thrusting into her, using hard punching movements. Easing off the pace though. He swiped the hair from her ear. "Stop thinking so hard." His voice was a deep rasp. "No thinking. You need to feel."

Page tried to talk but a moan slipped out instead.

"Do you feel me Page?" *Thrust. Thrust. Thrust.* Long. Hard. Deep.

"Yes," she sobbed.

"Because I feel you." *Thrust. Thrust. Thrust.* "Wet, Soft, fucking tight." His voice had a strained edge. "I could do this all day," he grunted. "All. Fucking. Day." He touched her hair, really softly. Her senses were in overload, goosebumps sprung up all over. *Thrust. Thrust. Thrust.* He picked up the pace and gripped a fistful of hair which he tugged backward, exposing her throat. The move was rough and yet tender. It was utterly dominating.

She couldn't move. In that moment, she couldn't think either. Could only feel as her body gave in to his demands. The coiling reached snapping point. She gulped for air and then wailed as an orgasm blasted through her. Mountain clutched her hair a little tighter which made her come harder. Even though her eyes were open, she saw nothing. She kept making the wailing noise but couldn't stop.

Mountain gave a startled yell and his hips jerked forwards as he grunted loudly. He kept up the thrusts for a time and then eased off, letting her hair go, as he slowed.

He finally pulled out and flipped her back over, lifting her into his arms. "I'm sorry, that came as a surprise." His chest heaved.

"Sorry for what?" She was still fighting to catch her breath as well. Page was frowning.

"For coming so quickly. It was just that... feeling you spasm around me..." His eyes were wide and he shook his head. "I could barely move... you squeezed the living shit out of me." He chuckled, still panting. "Felt so damned good."

"I'm still not getting the apology." Her voice sounded husky. He had held off for her. There was nothing to apologize for.

He picked her up, walking in the direction of the bedroom.

Page wrapped her legs around him.

"I planned on giving you two," he explained.

"Two what?" *Surely not?*

"Two orgasms. We'll rectify that right now." He touched his lips to hers for a second.

He was still completely deadpan. It wasn't a joke. "It's just that this was our first time." He was still apologizing. "It'll get better... much better."

"That was the best sex I've ever had." She may as well say it. "The best. I loved it."

He grinned and then his eyes turned stormy. "I want to be happy about that fact, but I can't. I'm going to make it my mission to blow your mind from here on out."

"Let's go to Vegas," she blurted. "Let's find Elvis and he can marry us right away. I love you so much. You're unbelievable. A dream come true."

He sat down on the edge of the bed. Page straddled

him. Mountain cupped her face. "I love you too." His eyes filled with emotion, making her eyes sting and her chest squeeze tight. "I want our mating ceremony to be special. Don't get me wrong, I don't want to wait either. Not long at any rate, but I want it to be an amazing day. A day we'll remember."

She smiled. "That sounds good." Then she thought of something. "Oh crap."

"What?" He narrowed his eyes in concern.

"You didn't use a condom. I mean, I'm on birth control, but look at what happened to Alex. I… we…"

Mountain smiled. "Hey," he murmured. "It's fine. We love each other. We're going to be mated soon."

"Very soon."

"Very soon," he agreed. "We love each other. I would love to have a couple of babies with you."

"Shew!" She nodded. "Okay, good, so we're not worried?"

"Not even a little bit." He brushed his lips over hers and then flipped her on her back. "You ready for round two?"

"Oh yes!" she laughed.

Mountain kissed her.

CHAPTER 20

Six weeks later...

Page looked over at Alex who was beaming. Her sister had the biggest smile on her face. Beck slid the ring onto her finger.

"No kissing yet," the elder—a dragon version of a minister—warned. He was also smiling.

Beck pretended to be put out and the audience erupted in laughs.

Alex giggled as she looked their way. "Your turn guys."

Beck also turned a little so that he faced them.

It was a double ceremony. Alex and Beck had just finished saying their vows. It was so sweet when Beck had gotten onto his knees to kiss Alex's rounded belly before proclaiming his undying love to Alex, who cried. A lot. She'd been doing a lot of that. Tearing up whenever she was happy, or nostalgic... heck, even when the kettle boiled, or a bird chirped, or a hat dropped. She blamed it on the hormones. Page believed it was all the years of having to hide her emotions. Now that she was free, she could express herself as much as she wanted, and express herself she did.

Page turned to face Mountain who took both her hands in his. She barely heard what the elder was saying for a half a minute. All she could see were Mountain's gorgeous chestnut eyes and the way they were focused on her. All she could feel was her incredible love for him. They made their promises to one another on a clifftop overlooking the ocean. All of their favorite people were there. His hair ruffled in the light breeze. He wore white cotton pants, his silver chest glinting in the sunlight. What could she say, he was so incredibly handsome it took her breath away. She had never been happier... and to think that this was just the start of it.

"Let the ring be a symbol of love." The elder looked uncomfortable. Dragons didn't exchange rings. This was purely a human tradition.

Mountain cleared his throat. After a few moments, he smiled. "One sec," he whispered, letting her hands go and turned to his brother. "This is the part where you give me the ring."

There were some snickers and laughs from the crowd. Mountain held his hand out to Obsidian who was frowning heavily.

Page bit down on her lip to keep from giggling. Obsidian handed Mountain the ring. He looked very uncomfortable and kept pulling on the waistband of his pants.

Shale winked at her from his position next to Obsidian.

Mountain turned back, his eyes serious, his jaw tight. He took her hand in his. "Love is too weak a word to even begin to describe how I feel about you, Page. I set out on that hunt wanting a female, any female. Little did I know that I would find you. My other half. My soul. No," he shook his head, "love is too tame when it comes to describing the fierce, unbridled passion I feel for you."

She sniffed, suddenly realizing that tears were tracking down her cheeks. Mountain wasn't the flowery, charming type. Everything he did or said came from a place of straight-down-the-line honesty. It meant more because of that. "I promise to be there always." He slid the ring onto her finger. The plain platinum band fit perfectly against her engagement ring. Mountain had picked out the biggest solitaire diamond she'd ever seen. It was beautiful. Nowhere near as beautiful as he was though.

"I can't wait to spend forever with you," she said through her tears. "Every day is going to be like a gift." Mountain cupped her cheeks with his big hands.

"Okay, you can kiss," the elder proclaimed. "I pronounce you mated," he quickly added. The poor guy had probably sensed that he didn't have much time left. That Mountain was going to kiss her anyway.

The crowd erupted but Page didn't hear a thing. She was too busy being swept off her feet. Quite literally, since her feet actually left the ground as he wrapped her in his arms and kissed her like there was no tomorrow.

Jenna was there as soon as he put her down. "Congrats!" Her friend hugged her.

"Thank you." Page had a huge grin plastered over her face.

"You did good," Jenna whispered in her ear. "So good," she added with a final squeeze, as she let go.

"I did, didn't I?" Her friend had approved of Mountain

from the moment she met him.

Jenna nodded.

"My turn." It was Deborah. It had been amazing to see her friend after all these years. In many ways, it was like they had never parted ways. Page and Debs hugged.

They were all helping the dragons as much as possible. Alex was the one who was in a position to impart the most information, and she had been as helpful as she could be. It hadn't taken long before the dragons began to accept her. The main problem was that none of them had been a part of the inner sanctum within the organization. So, their knowledge of the real workings within the group was limited. Alex had come to realize how little she really knew. It was all bigger picture stuff and no inner workings.

Their evening was something right out of a fairytale. From confetti to cake to the dancing and everything in between. Best of all, she got to share it with Alex and Beck. The four of them snuck out while the party was still in full swing.

"Did you ever in your wildest dreams think that this would be our lives one day?" Alex asked.

Page shook her head. "Nope, but things couldn't have turned out better."

"No, they couldn't have." She rubbed her belly. "You'll visit next week?" Alex raised her brows. She and Beck were headed for the Water lair, while Page and Mountain were going in the opposite direction to the Earth lair.

A little way to the left of them, Mountain chuckled and slapped Beck's back as they hugged. *What was going on over there?* she wondered, frowning and if she was honest, she was trying to listen in.

"Um," Alex touched the side of Page's arm to draw her

attention back, "Beck and I would love it if you could be our baby's godmother? Beck just asked Mountain about being the godfather and I take it that was a yes."

Page gasped and clasped a hand over her mouth. "Of course! I would... *we* would love it." She threw her arms around Alex's shoulders.

"Okay," Alex nodded, "it's settled then."

They said their goodbyes. The guys shifted and they headed home, which wasn't too far.

"I have something to show you," Mountain announced almost as soon as he shifted back into human form. "You ready?" he asked as he opened the door leading to their apartment. The lights were turned really dim.

"Yes." She smiled. "Although, you've given me so much already."

"Lights on," Mountain carefully articulated and true as Bob, the lights turned up bright. "Dim," he added, and they dimmed. "Lights off!" And bam... instead of switching off, they went right down to nightlight status. "See, they don't ever fully go off." He was smiling.

"Wow." She laughed. "That's great."

"Your turn." He took her hand.

"Lights on." Her voice sounded choked with emotion. Yet again, he was doing something kind for her. Showing how much he cared. "This means so much to me," she whispered.

"*You* mean so much to me." He squeezed her hand.

"No really." She shook her head, feeling her eyes well with tears. "You've never teased me. You've never complained." They slept with a night light on every night.

"I would never. Besides," he bobbed his eyebrows, "I like being able to see you every minute of every day."

"You can see in the dark, you dork." She rolled her eyes.

"I know but you look good bathed in the light." He winked at her and she laughed. Page had explained to Mountain how she'd developed night terrors after her mother died. She and Alex had been made to sleep in separate rooms. They were still so young. They hadn't been allowed to sleep with a light on. Or to get out of the bed. She'd have to lie there and try to work through her panic. She eventually reverted to wetting her bed. To screaming the house down. Her father had come up with an ingenious plan to 'cure' her. He decided she needed to be desensitized. He started locking her in a dark room for hours at a time. He wouldn't let her out, it didn't matter how much she screamed and begged. That she scratched at the door until her nail beds bled. The result – extreme and irrational fear of the dark. The condition had an actual name, nyctophobia. A phycologist she saw for a while told her it had, most likely, been brought on by separation anxiety when her mother passed. Her father's attempts at a cure had just made things worse.

"Your eyesight will improve now that we are mated," Mountain said. "We can keep the lights on as long as you need though."

"I know and thank you."

"The more sex we have, by the way," he kissed her on the forehead, "the quicker your senses will improve."

"Oh, really now?" She grinned up at him

"Oh yes, so I suggest we—" There was a knock at the door. "That's odd." Mountain frowned, his gaze on the door.

It was their wedding night. "That *is* odd," she agreed.

Another knock sounded. "Must be important."

Mountain's jaw tightened. "Good thing you're still dressed or—"

The person knocked again.

"I can hear it's Shale," Mountain announced. "He'd better not be fucking around, or I'll knock him out," he muttered as he headed for the door.

Page followed behind.

"What's up?" Mountain asked, as he opened the door.

Page peered around Mountain, getting a fright when she saw Shale's face.

"It's bad," Shale replied, his jaw was tight. His eyes had a strange look. Like he was afraid. She only ever knew Shale as a bit of a joker.

"Tell me," Mountain growled.

Shale swallowed thickly. "It's Obsidian. At least, we are almost certain it is him, since he is one of very few males unaccounted for. It sounds like it's him."

Mountain's twin had left hours ago, soon after the start of the party. No one had been worried though. Page had come to realize that such behavior could be expected from Obsidian.

"There's been an accident." Shale shook his head. "I mean, he's a little too in touch with his beast but... he wouldn't hurt someone would he?" His eyes got wide. "He wouldn't hurt a female?"

"What happened?" Mountain all but snarled.

"We don't know exactly. Only that a wolf Alpha's daughter went missing earlier. Would have been not too long after Obsidian left earlier."

"Wolf Alpha? What?" Mountain shook his head. "Where did this female go missing? What happened?"

"Blaze was contacted by Ward, one of the wolf alphas. Obsidian must have strayed into shifter territory—"

"But that's thousands of miles away." Mountain rubbed his jaw.

Shale shrugged. "A female is missing though. She's important to the wolves. She was promised to a bear Alpha… he's pissed. Her father is spitting bricks. Ward is beside himself."

"Did someone see him take her then? I can't believe Obsidian would do such a thing." Mountain's voice was a deep rasp.

"Who else would do this? And no, no one saw much of anything." He worked his jaw and flexed his muscles, looking like he was thinking something over.

"How do they know he took her? There's more. What are you not telling me?" Mountains muscles bulged.

Shale ran a hand through his hair. "There was blood. That's how they know. Both dragon and wolf blood, both of them were wounded. The area also scented strongly of rutting."

"What?" Mountain growled. "What are you saying? It doesn't make sense."

Page put her arms around his waist.

"They believe he forced himself on this poor female," Shale began.

Mountain growled. Page felt him tense.

"…that he has taken her against her will," Shale went on, his expression grave. "The shifters are out for blood."

"Oh no!" Page muttered.

"No." Mountain shook his head, looking distraught

"We are amassing a group to try to find them before the wolves and the bears do."

"I can't believe that Obsidian would do such a thing." Mountain shook his head again. His face was stricken. His eyes filled with concern. "I can't."

"I'm sorry." Page didn't know what else to say.

"I want to go with you," He said to Shale before he turned to her. "I have to go help find him before it's too late."

"Of course." She nodded. "I understand. Go." He barely touched his lips to hers and he was striding away.

END

AUTHOR'S NOTE

Charlene Hartnady is a USA Today Bestselling author. She loves to write about all things paranormal including vampires, elves and shifters of all kinds. Charlene lives on an acre in the country with her husband and three sons. They have an array of pets including a couple of horses.

She is lucky enough to be able to write full time, so most days you can find her at her computer writing up a storm. Charlene believes that it is the small things that truly matter like that feeling you get when you start a new book, or when you look at a particularly beautiful sunset.

BOOKS BY THIS AUTHOR

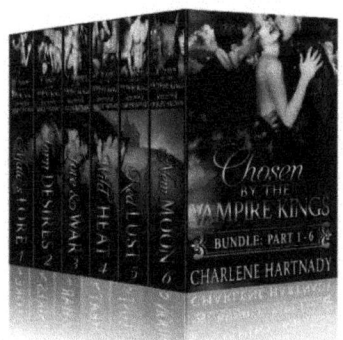

The Program Series (Vampire Novels)
Book 1 ~ A Mate for York
Book 2 ~ A Mate for Gideon
Book 3 ~ A Mate for Lazarus
Book 4 ~ A Mate for Griffin
Book 5 ~ A Mate for Lance
Book 6 ~ A Mate for Kai
Book 7 ~ A Mate for Titan

The Feral Series
Book 1 ~ Hunger Awakened
Book 2 ~ Power Awakened

Demon Chaser Series (No cliffhangers)
Book 1 ~ Omega
Book 2 ~ Alpha
Book 3 ~ Hybrid
Book 4 ~ Skin
Demon Chaser Boxed Set Book 1–3

The Bride Hunt Series (Dragon Shifter Novels)
Book 1 ~ Royal Dragon
Book 2 ~ Water Dragon
Book 3 ~ Dragon King
Book 4 ~ Lightning Dragon
Book 5 ~ Forbidden Dragon
Book 6 ~ Dragon Prince

The Water Dragon Series
Book 1 ~ Dragon Hunt
Book 2 ~ Captured Dragons
Book 3 ~ Blood Dragon
Book 4 ~ Dragon Betrayal

The Earth Dragon Series
Book 1 ~ Dragon Guard

Excerpt

Dragon HUNT

WATER DRAGONS BOOK 1

CHARLENE HARTNADY

CHAPTER 1

S he should be happy.

What was she thinking? She *was* happy.

Happy, excited and nervous all rolled into one. Nervous? Hah! She was quaking in her heels. This was a huge risk. Especially now. Her stomach clenched and for a second she wanted to turn around and head back into her boss's office. Tell him she'd changed her mind.

No.

She would regret it if she didn't take this opportunity. Why now though? Why had this fallen into her lap now? What if it didn't work out? She squeezed her eyes closed as her stomach lurched again.

"You okay?" Rob's PA asked, eyebrows raised.

Jolene realized she was standing outside her boss's office, practically mid-step. Hovering.

"Fine." She pushed out the word together with a pent-up breath. She *was* fine, she realized. More than fine, and she had this. The decision was already made. Her leave approved. She was doing this, dammit. Jolene smiled. "I'm great."

"Good." Amy smiled back. "Just so you know," she said under her breath, looking around them to check that no-one was in hearing distance, "I'm rooting for you." She winked.

"Thank you. I appreciate that," Jolene said as she headed back to her office, trying not to think about it. Not right now. It would make her doubt her decision all over again. She'd made the right one. The only thing holding her back was fear of failure. It was justifiable and yet stupid. She wasn't going to live with regrets because fear held her back. She was going to embrace this. Give it her all and then some. Her step suddenly felt lighter as she walked into her office. *Do not look left.* Whoever designed this building had been a fruitcake. This floor was large and open-plan. Fifty-three cubicles. There were only two offices. One was hers, and one was—*Not looking or thinking about her right now.* Both offices had glass instead of walls. Why bother? Why even give her an office in the first place if everyone could see into it?

It had something to do with bringing management closer to their staff, or the other way round – she couldn't remember. The Execs were on the next floor. *Not going there and definitely not looking left.* She could feel a prickling sensation on that side of her body. Like she was being watched. Jolene sat down at her desk and opened her laptop. Her accepted leave form was already in her inbox. She had to work hard not to smile. It was better to stay impassive. Especially when anyone could look in on her. This was going to work out. It would. All of it.

No more blind dates.

No more Tinder.

No more friends setting her up.

She was done! Not only was she done with trying to find a partner, she was done with human men in general. Jolene bit down on her bottom lip, thinking of the letter inside her purse. She'd been accepted.

Yes!

Whooo hooo!

It was all sinking in. She couldn't quite comprehend that this was actually happening.

The sound of her door opening snapped her attention back to the present. She lifted her head from her computer screen in time to see Carla saunter in. No knock. No apologies for interrupting. Not that Jolene had been doing anything much right then, but still. She could have been.

A smug smile greeted her. "I believe I'm filling in for you starting Friday for three weeks." Her colleague and biggest adversary sat down without waiting for an invitation. "Rob just called to fill me in."

"Yes," she cleared her throat, "that's right." Jolene nodded. *Don't let her get to you.* "I have too many leave days outstanding and decided to take them."

Carla folded her arms and leaned back. She seemed to be scrutinizing Jolene. It made her uncomfortable. "Yeah, but right now? You're either really sure of yourself or…" She let the sentence drop. "I believe you're going on a

singles' cruise?" The smirk was back. Carla's beady eyes—
not really, they were wide and blue and beautiful—were
glinting with humor and very much at Jolene's expense.

It was her own fault. She should never have told Rob
about why she was taking this trip. Why the hell had he
told Carla? It was none of her damned business. *Stay cool!*
She smiled, folding her arms. "I thought it would be fun."

"You do know that I'm about to close the Steiner deal,
right? Work on the Worth's Candy campaign is coming
along nicely as well."

"Why are you telling me this?" Her voice had a definite
edge which couldn't be helped. Carla irritated the crap out
of her.

The other woman shrugged. "It might not be the best
time for you to go on vacation. Not that I'm complaining.
It works for me." Another shrug, one-shouldered this
time.

Jolene pulled in a breath. "I need a break. That's the
long and short of it."

"Yeah, but right now and on a singles' cruise… do you
really think you'll meet someone?" She scrunched up her
nose.

"Why not? It's perfectly plausible that I would meet
someone. Someone really great!" she blurted, wanting to
kick herself for the emotional outburst.

"It's not like you have the greatest track record." Carla
widened her eyes. Unfortunately, working in such close
proximity for years meant that Carla knew a lot about her.
In the early days, they had even been friends.

"But you should definitely go," Carla went on. "You
shouldn't let that stop you," she quickly added. Her
comments biting.

"I'm not going to let anything stop me. Not in any aspect of my life," Jolene replied, thrilled to hear her voice remained steady.

Carla stood up, smoothing her pencil skirt. "I'll take care of things back here. The reason I popped in was to request a handover meeting, although I'm very much up to speed with everything that goes on around here." She gestured behind her. "I'll email a formal request anyway." She winked at Jolene.

Jolene had to stop herself from rolling her eyes. "Perfect." She refolded her arms, looking up at Carla who was still smiling angelically.

"I need you to know that I plan on taking full advantage of your absence."

"I know." Jolene smiled back. "I'm not worried."

The smile faltered for a half a second before coming back in full force. "You enjoy your trip. Good luck meeting someone." She laughed as she left. It was soft and sweet and yet grating all at once. Like the idea of Jolene actually meeting someone was absurd.

That woman.

That bitch!

Stay impassive. Do not show weakness. Do not show any kind of emotion. She forced herself to look down at her screen, to scroll through her emails.

Two minutes later, there was a knock at her door. Jolene looked up, releasing a breath when she saw who it was. Ruth smiled holding up two cups of steaming coffee.

Jolene smiled back and gestured for her to come in.

"I was in here Xeroxing—our printer is down yet again – and thought you could use a cup of joe." Ruth ran the admin department on the lower level. Her friend moved her eyeballs to the office next door to hers. The one where Carla sat, separated by just a glass panel.

"You were right," Jolene exclaimed.

Ruth sat down. "Are you okay? That whole exchange looked a little rough."

"I thought I kept my cool. Are you saying you could see how badly she got to me?" Carla was all about pushing buttons. She only won if Jolene retaliated and she'd learned a long time ago it wasn't worth doing so.

"You looked fine. What gave it away and – only because I know you so well – was the way you tapped your fingers against the side of your arm every so often. I take it when 'you know who' said something mean." Ruth handed her the coffee and took a seat.

"Mean doesn't begin to cut it. Thanks for this." She held up the mug before taking a sip.

"What's going on?"

"Things have happened so quickly, I didn't get a chance to tell you. I'm going on vacation." Jolene briefly told her friend all about her real upcoming plans, as well as about what had transpired between Carla and her.

Ruth smiled. "I can't believe you're this excited." She looked at her like she had lost all her faculties. "It's not that big of a deal. Quite frankly, I'm inclined to partly agree with Carla, for once." She made a face. "Maybe you shouldn't be going on a trip right now."

"It's a huge deal, and you're right, I'm excited," Jolene gushed. "One in five hundred applicants are accepted, and I'm one of them. The shifter program is just the place for a woman like me. I'm ready to settle down, to get married and to have kids. Lots of kids. Four or five… okay, maybe five's too many, but four has a ring to it. Two boys and two girls."

"Two of each." Ruth chuckled under her breath.

She smiled as well and shook her head. "Actually, I'm not too fazed about that. I just can't believe they actually selected me."

"You're nuts!" Ruth laughed some more. "Why's it so hard to believe? Just because you've had a bad run doesn't mean you're not… worthy."

"I'm thirty-four. I turn thirty-five in two months' time."

"And that's a big deal why?"

"Because thirty-five is the cut-off for taking part in the program." She had to undergo a whole lot of testing – including ones of the medical variety – and she'd been selected anyway. "I'm so done with guys running away as soon as they realize I'm serious."

"How is being a part of this program going to change anything? I love you long freaking time, but you do tend to scare men away. You're a little… pushy."

"I'm not pushy! I know what I want and I go after it. After everything I've been through, I'm not interested in anything less, and shifters actually want to settle down. They want kids. They want what I want. For once, I'm going to meet someone who doesn't run scared at the prospect of commitment and family." She sucked in a deep breath.

"Human guys also want commitment." Ruth raised her brows, taking another sip of her coffee. "They want kids."

"Just not with me they don't. None of them wanted anything other than sex or casual dating. Sure, they're more than willing to take the plunge as soon as they move on to the next one, but not with me."

"Have you ever stopped to consider that you're maybe

coming on just a little too strong? You can't start out a relationship talking about marriage. Guys can't handle that."

"I'm not coming on too strong. I'm done wasting my time… that's all." Jolene took a sip of her own coffee, feeling the warm liquid slide down her throat. "I know what I want. Casual sex, endless dating…" She shook her head. "That's not it. Even living together. Have you ever heard the saying, 'why buy the cow if you can get the milk for free'? No… not for me. Never again!"

"You seem to think it's going to be different with a shifter. Can't say I know too much about shifters." Ruth shrugged. "Except that they're ultimately guys too."

"For starters they're hot. Muscular, tall and really, really good-looking."

"Okay, that's a good start." Ruth leaned forward, eyes on Jolene.

"They have a shortage of their own women, just like with the vampires. It's actually the vampires who are helping them set up this whole dating program."

"Oh!" Ruth looked really interested at this point. "No women of their own you say, now that's interesting."

"I didn't say no women, just not many women. Their kind stopped having female children, so there's a shortage. They have a natural drive to mate and procreate, which is exactly what I'm looking for." Jolene put her coffee down and rubbed her hands together. "I can't wait to get my hands on one."

"You might just be onto something here. Where do I sign up?" her friend whisper-yelled while smiling broadly. "I can't believe you told Rob you're going on a cruise. Where did you come up with that?"

"I shouldn't have said anything at all." She shook her head. "I don't know why I disclosed as much as I did."

"Yeah!" Ruth raised her brows. "I can't believe he told," she looked to the side while keeping her head facing forwards, "her."

"I know. Thing is, I've made up my mind. I'm going."

"That cow is going to move in while you're gone. She might just get the edge in your absence and take the promotion out from under you."

"I realize that, and yet I can't miss out on this opportunity. I'm willing to risk my career over this. It's a no-brainer for me." She sighed. "Don't get me wrong, I'm freaking out about it, but as much as I love my job, having a family would trump everything. I have a good feeling about this."

"Those shifters sound so amazing." Ruth bobbed her brows.

"I'll show you the website online. They only take three groups a year and then only six women are chosen each time. Just a handful from thousands of applications." Jolene's heartbeat all the faster for getting accepted. She was so lucky! Things had to work out for her. They just had to.

"You say these shifters are hot and pretty desperate?" Ruth smiled, her eyes glinting. "Why didn't you tell me about this sooner? We should have entered together."

"Not exactly desperate, but certainly looking for love. Ninety-six percent of the women who sign up end up mated... that's what the shifters call it, mated. It's not actually the same as marriage, it's more binding. Ninety-six percent," she shook her head, "I rate those odds big time."

"I can't believe you didn't tell me sooner." Even though she was still smiling, Ruth narrowed her eyes. "I thought we were friends."

Jolene made a face. "I didn't tell you anything because I didn't want to jinx it."

Ruth rolled her eyes. "I wouldn't get too excited until you get there. Until you actually meet them." Ruth snickered. "With your luck, you'll get one of the bad apples."

"You shut your mouth. Don't be putting such things out in the universe."

Ruth looked at her with concern. "I don't want you getting your hopes up, that's all."

"Well too late, my hopes are already up." Jolene was going to win herself a shifter. Someone sweet and kind and loving. A man she could spend forever with. "I just wish it wasn't right now. This isn't a good time to be leaving."

"Not with that big promotion on the horizon." Ruth shook her head. "Not when *she* could take it."

"We're both on the same level. We both started at the same time. I hate how evenly matched we are."

"You're the better candidate though. I've never known anyone to work as hard as you."

"Carla works hard too. She's also brought in several big clients in the last couple of months, and she's not going on vacation. She'll be here day in and day out, whispering sweet nothings into Rob's ear."

Ruth made a face. "It's not like that, is it?"

"No, no." She waved a hand. "Sweet nothings of the business kind. It's still a threat just the same to me, and honestly, that's the only downside to this. I stand a good chance of losing to Carla if I go."

"But you are still going anyway." Ruth took a sip of her coffee, frown lines appearing on her forehead.

"I have to." She pushed out a breath. Hopefully, Ruth was wrong about the whole 'bad apple' thing.

Out now!

Lightning Source UK Ltd.
Milton Keynes UK
UKHW011826170619
344563UK00001B/244/P